The Firefighter
And The Girl From
The Coffee Shop

By

Terry Towers

The Firefighter And The Girl From The Coffee Shop

Chapter 1

"You only have a week left Alyssa, then he's fair game."

With annoyance welling within her Alyssa Thornton narrowed her dark eyes and glared over her shoulder at Samantha. Her attention was turned back to the task at hand; admiring one of the most magnificent things she'd ever seen through the side pane glass window of the coffee shop, while pretending to wipe down the tables in the dining room. Evan Saunders.

Evan was the newest firefighter employed at the station across the street. And like her, he usually worked the overnight shift. The girls at the coffee shop had a rule, you must "claim" a man you're interested in. This would make him off limits to the other girls at the shop and you were given a month to seal the deal with him otherwise he came up for grabs again.

Alyssa claimed Evan from the second she laid eyes on him, but there seemed to be a slight problem... Over the past few weeks - nearing a month - they seemed to have established a good, solid *friendship.*

"Ta ta ladies," Samantha purred as she exited the coffee shop, after finishing her eight hour shift, leaving Alyssa and her co-worker Jenny to work the overnight shift.

As Samantha strutted across the parking lot to her vehicle, Jenny - a no non-sense woman in her mid-fifties - came up behind Alyssa to stand beside her. While watching Evan as she pretended to assist with cleaning the dining room. "You realize as soon as the week is up, she'll be on him faster than you can blink."

Alyssa groaned. Yeah, she knew all too well that Samantha would literally pounce on him the minute her week was up. Samantha was the equivalent of a piranha when it came to men. She got whomever she wanted and devoured them fast, moving on to the next one. And sweet, sexy-as-sin Evan was very succulent prey.

"Do you want me to talk to him for you? All I had to do was give Jade a little push and look how it turned out for her."

"Yes, I know, she's engaged now." Alyssa sighed. She was happy for her, Jade was a sweet girl. In a few weeks Jade would be tying the knot with "Officer Hottie," as he was known as around the coffee house, an absolute dream of a man. She turned and wagged her finger at Jenny. "I don't want you interfering. I'm twenty-eight for heaven's sakes, I think I can wrangle up my own date."

A grin touched Jenny's lips and she raised a sceptical brow at Alyssa. "All I know is that my ninety year old grandmother can snag a man in less time then it has taken you to build up enough courage to ask him. This isn't the fifties anymore Alyssa. Women *can* make the first move now."

Crossing her arms over her chest Alyssa cocked her head and eyed her co-worker. "First of all, I've met your grandmother and that woman is spry for her age. And secondly, I've given the signals."

"Signals?"

"Yeah." She reached out and touched Jenny's arm lightly. "Like gently touching his arm or shoulder, you know, establishing physical contact."

"Uh-huh."

"Asking leading questions dropping subtle hints. He'd just not really interested I guess. Alyssa gave a long sigh before admitting her biggest fear to Jane. I think I've been shouldered into the friend zone."

Jane gasped, this was every girl's nightmare. "Oh God, we definitely don't want that." Planting a fist on her hip Jenny gave Alyssa a stern look and pointed a long slender finger over at Evan. "You see that man over there."

Alyssa glanced over and her eyes took in the sight of him: tall, large, powerful build, short cut dark brown hair and deep green eyes. And his voice... he had a deep, powerful voice that made her melt. Yeah, she saw him, most evenings she spent a good chunk of time watching him from afar like some love struck teenager.

"Yeah, I see him... And."

Wagging her finger in his direction Jenny clucked her tongue off the roof of her mouth and shook her head. "That man does *not* put women in the 'friend zone,' as you young people like to call it. Either you're giving off some fucked up signals that's making him unsure about you or he's already involved with someone..."

"Nah," Alyssa shook her head, "he's not with someone already. I already know that much."

Shrugging, Jenny picked up the dishrag from the table she'd just finished wiping down and turned to walk back to the kitchen. "In that case you're doing something wrong. He's interested. He wouldn't be coming over here to chat with you several times a night just for the fun of it. If you know what I mean.".".

"You need to make your move Alyssa, time's ticking. Tick -tock, tick- tock."

Jenny huffed as she walked away not bothering to look back.

Alyssa sighed, as she contemplated on all what Jenny had told her. A ding sounded in the earpiece of her drive-thru headset signalling a customer at the speaker. She rushed to the drive-thru section, her usual station for the majority of the night, as she pressed the TALK button on the control box, hooked to her belt and asked to take their order.

****

"Visit number one of the night coming up," Jenny announced over the headset as Alyssa came out of the walk-in freezer with an armful off meats to prep the sandwich bar with. She glanced over her shoulder at the clock in the kitchen as she passed by it and noticed it was slightly early for him to be showing up. It wasn't even two hours into her shift yet. A shiver of anticipation rushed through as she quickened her pace to deposit the food in the cooler up front so she could meet him outside for her first break.

"Do you mind if-"

Jenny rolled her eyes and grinned. "Go ahead. But for the love of God get a date out of the man already."

Alyssa returned the older woman's grin as she removed her headset, dark brown visor, and hairnet and then shook her long dark locks free of the clip holding them into a loose bun at the back of her head. "How do I look?"

Jenny snorted. "Good. Same as you do every other night."

A bang on the side window, courtesy of Evan, had Alyssa rushing to the side door. "I'll be back in fifteen," she called over her shoulder as she unlocked the side door and stepped out into the warm summer night air.

"I know I'm early tonight. Bored." Evan crossed his arms over his broad chest and reclined against the brick wall of the coffee shop.

Damn, he's sexy. "Isn't that a good thing?" she asked, closing the door behind her and standing a couple feet away from him, her hands stuffed into her back pockets.

Evan huffed then gave her the sexy, dimpled smile that sent her heart racing each time she saw it. "Yeah, I suppose. I can only handle playing cards for so long though. Ralph is in a mood because his wife left him-"

"Again?"

Evan shrugged, "-And Jeremy is studying for some college exam he has to take next week and well... you *know* that Troy and I do not get along. So..."

"So, you might as well spend some time chatting with the coffee shop girl huh?"

His grin deepened. "Something like that." He jerked his thumb in the direction of the firehouse, "Besides you're a hell of a lot more pleasing to the eyes than those clowns over there."

Alyssa's brow furrowed. "Thanks. I think..."

He raked a hand through his hair and sighed. "Yeah, and a... there is this thing coming up next month."

"A thing?" her heart leaped at the thought that he might finally ask her out on a date.

"Yeah, like an annual city wide fireman's ball thing. It's a formal thing."

"Formal ball thing huh?" Alyssa teased as she rocked back on her heels and her dark eyes caught his. So was he simply sharing the information for the sake of conversation, or was he hinting? Damn it! She hated having to read between the lines, if there were lines to be read between. She groaned inwardly. How she wished she had the confidence of Samantha, to simply see a man she wanted and go and get him. Life would be so much easier, at least when it came to men anyhow.

But she wasn't Samantha.

He paused not saying anything more for close to a minute, as if waiting for her to say something more about it; when she didn't he shrugged. "Yeah, will probably just offer to work it so the other guys can go."

Alyssa heart sank. For one glistening moment she thought he was finally going to break the ice and ask her out. But nope, instead she feared she'd just sunk a little deeper into the friend zone with him. She silently cursed herself for letting the opportunity pass her by.

Frowning, he pushed himself off of the wall and took a step towards her, his massive frame towering over hers. "What have you been doing in there? You have a little something..." he slowly, hesitantly, touched the side of her cheek with his hand, his thumb grazing her jaw, wiping away the smudge.

Closing her eyes, Alyssa sighed basking in the soft caress. She could feel him moving closer, and his breath intermingled with hers. When she opened her eyes back up, they immediately locked onto his hunger filled ones, his mouth mere inches away. She could feel the heat rising between them, like a simmering fire, waiting for the ideal moment to rage out of control.

She felt her cheeks growing warm.

Thinking back she remembered that before cleaning the dining room she was powdering some of the donuts so she must have gotten some on herself. She was like a little tornado of disaster; wherever she went, whatever she touched, became a disaster in virtually every aspect of her life. A prime example, aside from the powder on her chin was the man standing before her. All she needed to do was take a chance, lean into him and let the chips fall as they may... It seemed like such a simple and easy thing to do.

They stood, gazing into each others eyes, their breaths continuing to mix until their breathing became synchronized. Both longed to make the contact, but neither one was willing to take the risk.

Headlights passed by, breaking the moment - and she noticed a couple of cars entering the parking lot, heading for the drive-thru speaker. Stepping back she ran a shaky hand through her long dark hair and shrugged, giving him an apologetic smile. "I gotta go. I'm sorry. I think the bar rush is beginning." Walking over to the side door she grabbed the handle, and then turned back to him. "See you later?"

Hesitating a moment, he straightened to his full six-foot-three and nodded, thrusting his hands into the pockets of his black pants. "Yeah, I ummm." He nodded and let out a loud huff of air, "I'll be back later."

Pulling open the door, Alyssa slipped inside giving him a small wave as she locked it behind her. She watched him turn and saunter off across the street, her eyes admiring his broad, muscular back and tight ass. She could only imagine how amazing his body would look naked. In fact, she imagined it frequently whenever she lay in bed pleasuring herself.

"The *ass man* wants a BLT," Jenny called out to her as she made her way back behind the counter.

"The *ass man*." Alyssa groaned as she put her hair back up in a bun and put her headset back on. Just who she wanted to see, the ass man. The ass man was a taxi driver who was infamous for openly ogling the women at the coffee shop. His favourite trick was to wait until he got to the window and then request something the coffee shop girl would have to bend over to get so he could get a good look at her rump.

"That's a BLT, on wheat please."

Hustling over to the sandwich bar she began to put the sandwich together. "I'm not letting him look at my ass tonight."

Jenny laughed and gave Alyssa a wink over her shoulder. "I'll let him look at mine instead. Better?"

"Much. Thanks."

With her back to the drive-thru window Alyssa didn't see his smirk, but knew he was wearing one as the Ass man's cab pulled up to the window and he greeted them with his usual 'how's my fine girls tonight.' She didn't have to look to know his eyes were inspecting her ass as she made his sandwich.

"Hey, Alyssa honey, you want to bend down there and get me an extra creamer from the cooler."

Alyssa gritted her teeth. "Sure Richard, not a problem at all." Bending over she slid the cooler door open and grabbed a couple creamer packets from inside.

A whistle sounded from the window. "Looking mighty fine tonight Alyssa honey."

Her blood boiled as her pink face turned bright red with anger, she had to do something to help her calm down. Alyssa took a deep breath in and released it, counting backwards from ten slowly in her head.

Straightening up she took a moment to daydream about chucking the creamer at his perverted little head as she wrapped up his sandwich and thrust it into a paper bag. By the time Alyssa made it to the window Jenny had already finished the rest of his order and had taken his payment.

"Enjoy." Alyssa tossed the sandwich at him with a little too much force. It slammed into his chest and then fell to his lap.

"Oh, she's feisty tonight isn't she?" he turned his attention over to Jenny for confirmation and grinned; not in the slightest bit concerned that she'd just tossed his food at him or that he may have offended her.

"Yeah, she's got some issues she's working on."

With a curt nod, Richard put the car into gear and sped off, promising to see them again later.

Can't wait, Alyssa thought as she watched the taillights of his car disappear around the corner and out of sight.

Planting a hand on her hip, Jenny turned and glowered at Alyssa. "You are a thousand shades of pathetic you know that?"

"Huh?" Alyssa frowned as she turned to face her friend.

"I saw what happened out there with Evan."

"You were snooping?" A look of disbelief swept across Alyssa's face.

"I was *evaluating* so I could help, and what I saw was..." she shook her head in disgust. "Do you *want* to be single the rest of your life?"

Alyssa's frown deepened. "What do you mean?"

"The man was pretty much *begging* you to kiss him and you just brushed him off."

Alyssa gulped. "Jenny, come on."

"Don't you know a hint when you hear one? Maybe if I'd been listening to you two all along, you guys would have been together already." She sighed, shaking her head. "I don't know what you've said to him over these past few weeks, but ten to one he thinks he doesn't have a shot with you, but bless his sexy ass he's trying."

"But he just *mentioned* the firemans' ball and I *did* have flour on my chin!" She protested as Jenny gave her one more disgusted look and brushed past her. "And that was kind of mean of you , by the way!"

"Tough love baby. I'm just calling it like I see it," Jenny responded disappearing into the kitchen to continue with her cleaning.

"I did have a smudge..." She grumbled as she grabbed a stack of cups from the under counter cabinet, removed the plastic covering them and thrust them violently into cup dispenser. "A thousand shades of pathetic my ass."

As much as she hated to admit it, Jenny was right.

Chapter 2

"Alyssa not working tonight?" Ralph asked as he and Evan stepped outside for a breath of cool night air.

It was another slow night and it seemed even slower without Alyssa next door at the coffee shop to visit every couple of hours to help break up the night. Evan leaned back against the cold brick of the firehouse wall and sighed. "Nah, she took the night off. Had something to do that was going to take most of the day, I guess." He shrugged.

"So why haven't you asked her out?" Reclining next to Evan, Ralph chuckled "Or have you asked and she rejected you?"

"No. She hasn't *rejected* me. I haven't asked. Well, not really anyhow. I'm waiting for the right moment."

"Bah, maybe you need a little of the Latino charm, brother."

"Hmmm, didn't your wife just leave you the other day?"

Ralph grinned. "Oh, I didn't tell you? She came back this morning, was waiting for me when I came home." He gave Evan a wink. "She couldn't stay away from her Cuban stallion."

"Oh really, I was wondering why your mood was so good tonight."

"So why haven't you made a move for the coffee house girl."

"Well, we never talk about it, but I heard she was involved with someone already. Strange, she never mentions him, but that doesn't mean it's not true."

"Did you ask her?"

"Nah, hinted about the fireman's ball though."

"No bites."

Evan shook his head. "Not even a nibble." Evan thought back to the previous night he'd hinted towards asking her to the ball and she didn't even appear to be interested in going with him. He then brought about a situation where all she had to do was meet him halfway. She just needed to move a fraction of an inch towards him and it would have been all the motivation he needed to make the move he'd been aching to make from the first day they'd met.

Instead, she ran off as fast as she could to serve the asshole in the cab. That should have told him everything he needed to know, but the problem was that he felt the connection between them. Maybe he was crazy, maybe it was all in his head. He'd just moved to Portland a month ago and hadn't been on a date in a number of months. Perhaps he was starting to get rusty and was reading the signals wrong. Maybe he was mistaking her kindness for something more than just friendship, when friendship was all it really was?

"Do you think maybe your past couple of relationships may be keeping you from pursuing this one?"

Evan frowned and snorted at Ralph. "What? When the fuck did you become Dr. Phil?"

"Well the truth hurts brother"

Evan ran the scenario quickly through his mind. His two previous relationships had ended in almost the same way. The women had gotten annoyed with his long work hours and so they decided to take on extracurricular activities - with other men. The second one even had the nerve to take her other boyfriend to their house and fuck him in *his* bed! Yes, Ralph could probably be right; maybe he was being slightly standoffish with Alyssa. But it was with good reasoning, after what had happened between him and these two women, he would be damned if he let another woman hurt or betray him. It almost seemed like he was on a roll with these failed relationships. A roll he wasn't overly eager to continue.

But Alyssa was different. His gut told him she was and he was inclined to believe it. But still... Yeah, maybe the Cuban Dr Fucking Phil standing beside him had a point.

He didn't have much time to ponder it further because the alarm inside the firehouse sounded and there was a flurry of shouts and activity inside. Without hesitation both men rushed into the station and began to get ready. Within a couple of minutes the fire truck was in motion and all men - Evan included, were on their way to put out a fire in an apartment building several blocks away.

****

Alyssa awoke to an ear piercing buzzing and smoke filling her lungs. She coughed violently as she opened her eyes and sat up. The room had gotten incredibly hot and a thick cloud of smoke lined the air.

Oh-my-God. Fire! Alyssa stumbled from the bed, again being overtaken by another violent bout of coughing, causing her to drop to her knees on the floor. *Need to get out!* Looking down at herself wearing an extremely sheer pink lacy teddy she very briefly considered changing her clothing, but screams coming from the floor below her prompted her to start moving, crawling towards the bedroom door as quickly as she could managed, reasoning that she'd rather be seen partially naked by the neighbours than dead.

As she quickly made her way out of the bedroom and into the living room she gasped, seeing that the bathroom attached to the living room was already up in flames. "Oh God, oh God." She said in a panicked voice, rubbing her fingers viciously against her smoke burnt eyes. She stumbled to her feet frantic to get out and was hit with another fit of coughing that brought her back down to her knees. The stiffening in her lungs got more intense causing her to grip hard onto her chest, as she tried desperately to breathe through the heavy mass of smoke. It was so hot that her sweat was causing the thin material of her teddy to cling to her ivory skin.

Her eyes perused her space trying to find an opening to make her escape. She had the worst feeling ever, would this be her end? Her thoughts were stopped short with the sudden sound of banging at her door. Then a male voice called out to her, but her throat was now so sore she could barely speak. Her coughing felt like razor blades were ripping her throat apart from the inside out and she was beginning to feel dizzy and extremely faint. She noticed her purse and snatched it from the side table as she once more stumbled to her feet.

A whooshing sound came from her bathroom and she yelped as the fire overtook the bathroom completely and began to creep into the kitchen. Alyssa stumbled another few feet and collapsed just as her front door came crashing in and a couple of firemen came rushing in.

"Oh Jesus! It's Alyssa!" she heard a familiar voice say just as the light-headed feeling took over once more and she found herself giving into the darkness as she clung to the strap of her brown leather handbag...

****

She wasn't sure how long she was out, but when she came around she was on a gurney in the back of an ambulance. "Where, what?" She tried to sit up, but her head felt as though it had been hit with a sledgehammer and her throat burned with such intensity that she could not even speak a word.

A large, strong hand took hers bringing her attention to the person to the left of her. A smile touched her lips as she noticed Evan sitting next to her. He was suited up, soot smeared across his face and clothing and looking sexier than she'd ever seen him.

"Y-you s-saved." she managed to get out, then coughed and groaned lying back onto the gurney and closing her eyes.

He gave her hand a slight squeeze. "You're going to be okay, you just need to rest a little while, and here..."

She slowly opened her eyes to see him passing her a glass of water. "Come on. Take a drink."

He helped her into a sitting position, keeping a hand between her shoulder blades to keep her steady as he brought the glass to her lips.

Covering his hands with hers, she drank a couple of swallows and pulled away as another fit of coughing overtook her.

"Thank you," she managed to squeak out as she looked over at him, just in time to see where his eyes had been. Frowning, she looked down and realized that combination of sweat with the already sheer material had made it virtually transparent; her large beige nipples were tight and completely visible through the teddy. She grabbed the end of the blanket covering her and pulled it up to her chin.

"I ummm." Despite the soot covering a good portion of his face, she was amused to see him flush, from being caught sneaking a peek.

Taking the water from him once more she took another couple of sips and was relieved to find the soreness was lessoning - slightly. "Was anyone hurt?"

Evan shook his head, "Nah, we got everyone out in time and I think you're going to be fine. Is there someplace I can take you? Family member," he paused, "boyfriend?"

Alyssa shook her head to both suggestions, and thought she saw a look of flicker in his green eyes. "My family is from Bangor and right now isn't the best time anyhow my aunt passed away. Today was the funeral."

Evan frowned, as he leaned forward bracing his elbows on his knees and lacing his fingers. "So no boyfriend?"

A soft smile touched her lips as she shook her head. "None." She shrugged, "I just got paid and have a few dollars in the bank... Rent is due tomorrow, but I don't think I'll be paying it so I can just go to a hotel until I figure something better out."

He caught her eyes with him, concern flashing in them. "What about friends."

Again she shook her head, her amble unrestrained breasts swaying slightly with the movement, which caught his eyes briefly before he pulled them back up to meet hers again. "No one I'd ask. You've been pretty much my closest friend since I moved here. Remember, I'm also new to the area, got here just a month or so before you did."

Evan remained silent for a moment, and then smiled over at her. "Then stay with me. I have a three bedroom house and live alone so there is lots of room for you." He looked down at her soiled teddy. "And I might even be willing to lend you some clothing. It'll be big on you, but it'll do until we can get you to a store tomorrow. Hell, we both have the next couple of days off so we can take a day for it."

She was about to protest and tell him she didn't want to intrude or impose, but then it occurred to her that if ever there was a chance to be with him, this was it. They could get to know each other on a day-to-day basis and perhaps break through the invisible barrier that seemed to be keeping them from moving the relationship from friendship to something more.

She returned his smile. "Well if I wouldn't be a bother..."

"You wouldn't."

"So there's no girlfriend to get angry." *Please say no, please say no.* She was ninety-nine percent sure he didn't, but just wanted to make sure she was clear - just in case.

He laughed, his eyes lit up with the smile that followed. "Nah, no worries on that."

She thrust out her hand to him. "Then you have yourself a roomie."

Laughing a little harder, his eyes shining with amusement he accepted her hand, giving it a firm shake. "Roomie it is."

****

With the fire resistant blanket wrapped tightly around her, Alyssa followed Evan into the quaint two-story house he owned on the outskirts of the city. Her first impression was how neat and tidy it was, everything in its place and not a speck of dust or clutter to be found. Evan was certainly a man of simplicity and organization, something she hadn't quite realized until that moment.

"The bedrooms are upstairs. Come on up and I'll get you some clothes."

Removing the blue slippers given to her by the fire department she left them at the door and padded barefoot up the stairs after him to the second floor. He stopped at the first door and waved her in.

"Boxers and a t-shirt okay?" he asked as he brushed past her, making his way to the large oak dresser across the room.

"That would be great, thank you." Alyssa surveyed the room. As with the rest of the house it was simple, yet cosy. The room and decor were all of an eye catching burgundy colour. The bedroom set was made of varnished oak, with the massive bed taking up a good chunk of the room. "Everything is so... orderly."

Evan turned to face her closing the dresser drawer with his hip, a pair of plain boxers and white t-shirt in his hand. He gave a light chuckle and his eyes swept the room. "Yeah, both of my parents are in the army. Both officers. I lived in a house where tidiness and order were the gospel," he shrugged as he strode over to her and started to pass her the clothing and then stopped. "You know what? How about you grab a shower. You can use the one here and I'll run downstairs and use the main one."

Hmmmm, a shower. With the craziness of the night, it hadn't even occurred to her that she must look and smell nasty. Taking a strand of hair she brought it to her nose and cringed at the burnt smell. Yes, a shower was definitely in order.

She smiled warmly, heat rising to her cheeks thinking of how horrid her appearance must be at that moment.

He tossed the clothing to the bed, "When you're done and changed I'll give you an official tour." Without waiting for a reply he brushed past her, and left the room closing the door behind him.

Dropping the blanket, she shed her soot covered teddy and panties as she made her way to the bathroom off the master bedroom. Snatching the filthy clothing from the floor she considered saving them and having them washed, but upon taking a hard look at the blackened material she decided against it and tossed them into the waste basket next to the flush.

As with the rest of the house, Alyssa found the bathroom to be bright and sparkling clean, however, she couldn't help but snicker when she noticed the shower curtain that was pastel blue in colour, featuring a cartoon duck wearing a purple raincoat, boots and holding an umbrella.

Pulling the curtain aside she turned on the shower and stepped into the tub. Alyssa sighed as she let the soft stream of warm water beat against her back. She immediately began to relax, as the beads of water caressed her skin. Looking down at her feet she was shocked to see the water was near black from the soot and smoke.

"No wonder he suggested the shower. I'm a damned mess," she grumbled grabbing a facecloth, squeezing a dab of shower gel onto it and beginning to scrub down her body, removing the black to reveal ivory skin underneath. Her hair was a little harder to get clean; it took several shampoos before she noticed the water running clear down her body.

She could have stayed in the shower for hours, but the sound of Evan moving around below her made her realize he was already done and would be back up to check on her soon. Rinsing the last of the conditioner from her hair, she turned off the tap, grabbed a towel and stepped out of the shower wrapping the blue towel around her body, and then wrapping a second towel around her long, dark locks.

Quickly, she made her way out of the bathroom and into the bedroom. She grabbed the t-shirt he had given her and slipped it over her head and then stepped into the boxers. Fisting the front of the shirt she closed her eyes, brought it to her nose and inhaled. Damn it smelt good, like him, a mixture of musk and spice. Just the smell of him on the clothing caused a stirring with her.

She was adjusting the drawstring to the boxers when her eye caught sight of the dress uniform hanging from a hook over his closet door. She immediately went over to the impressive looking uniform and was inspecting it, when a knock came at the door and Evan cautiously opened it a crack. "You dressed?"

"Sorry. Yes." She glanced at him over her shoulder and then back to the uniform. "You decided to go to the ball after all?" She heard him walk up behind her and felt the warmth of breath against her neck, which sent a pleasurable shiver through her.

"I'm still thinking on it. As it is right now I'm without a date and not keen on attending it alone."

She spun around and took a moment to admire his naked broad, beautifully toned chest. The lines from his six-pack abdominals and the way his plaid flannel bottoms sat low on his hips, caused her eyes to dip lower than they should have to the large bulge beneath is bottoms. Her entire body seemed to ignite and she began to feel an uncomfortable wetness between her legs.

"Haven't you asked anyone?" She reluctantly pulled her eyes up from admiring his stunning body and gave him a sly smile, catching her lower lip between her teeth and nibbling nervously. "I'm sure there's a line of women waiting for you to make a move." She was hoping to sound as nonchalant as possible, but feared that she did a terrible job at it.

He took a step closer, closing the distance between them and leaving just a little over an inch between their bodies. "Well, I had someone specific in mind to take with me, but I've been getting the feeling that they aren't all that interested."

Evan's green eyes seemed to burrow into her, fuelling her yearning for him. She wished she could get over her insecurities and just take a chance. He wasn't attached; she knew one hundred percent now. He wanted her, it was becoming painfully apparent. Why couldn't she just take the step and bridge the small gap left between them?

"Well maybe you need to be a little more aggressive about getting what you want?" She swept her tongue along her lower lip, leaving it shining, begging for him to kiss her. His eyes dropped to her mouth, following her tongue as he looked down at them hungrily. Gathering up her courage she continued, "Maybe she's had some bad experiences in the past and perhaps she's a little timid about assuming anything. Maybe she needs you to be more direct."

His eyes rose back up to meet hers once more. "I would hope that this person would have been able to see how crazy I am for her. If I hadn't been told she was dating someone then perhaps I would have been."

Been told I was dating someone? By who? The question had just entered her mind when the answer came directly after it. *Samantha!* She pressed down the anger welling up within her. She'd have a chat with Samantha when she went back to work. At the moment she had more important things to contend with and that being Evan as he closed the remaining distance between them, his lips lightly grazing hers.

"Evan," she managed to whisper as his lips came crashing down onto hers and his still wet rock hard body pressed against her, pushing her back against the closet door with a little more force than intended.

****

There were a hundred different thoughts and emotions rushing through Evan as he lowered his lips to Alyssa's and finally took the one thing that he'd been wanting for nearly a month. His first thought was how wonderful she smelt and how damned sexy she looked in his t-shirt and boxers which were a couple of sizes too big on her.

And that moan... She moaned softly against his lips as he claimed them. The sound was so soft and sensual that it sent his cock into a frenzy as it rose rapidly under the thin fabric of his pants. He braced a palm flat on the wall beside her head and the other one snaked it way to the back of her head and threaded itself into her hair, pulling her lips up tighter to his.

He was attempting to keep as much separation between their bodies as possible, so he could keep himself under control, but Alyssa slipped her hands around his waist and pulled him in, closer than he had ever been to her. His stiff cock pressed against her stomach and he groaned. He'd wanted her for so fucking long; he had fantasized - hell, jacked off - to thoughts of what it would be like to taste and feel her soft body against his. And now he knew, and it was everything he imagined it to be.

She parted her lips for him, allowing his tongue entry into her sweet mouth. He eagerly accepted the invitation his tongue finding and caressing hers. She pulled him tighter, her hips pressing against him, taunting his cock, and turning his body into a tight bundle of nerves. His fists clenched in her hair as he tore his lips from hers, and began to nibble his way along her jaw.

At that moment he'd have given just about anything to tear his clothing from her body and ram his dick hard into her. Her sweet little pussy would take him in eagerly, clinging to his cock and enticing him to remain there embedded in her moist heated core. He shuttered at the thought.

"My God Evan!" she gasped as she arched her back, and exposed her neck for his hungry mouth and teasing tongue.

Evan began to kiss his way down her neck, his tongue teasing, flicking at the sensitive flesh as he worked his way lower. She pressed up against him once more and in turn pushing the limits of his self-restraint. He had gotten down to her collarbone and the collar of his t-shirt when his home phone began to ring.

"Awww fuck! I gotta answer that," he growled, before kissing her quickly on the lips once more and pushing himself away from her. He didn't have the luxury of ignoring the telephone, the station may need him, someone may have gotten sick, perhaps another fire that needed more men. He never knew.

"Okay." she managed to squeak out, her chest heaving, eyes hooded.

"Give me a quick second."

Alyssa nodded, watching him as he turned his back to her and picked up the receiver.

Chapter 3

Oh-my-God. Alyssa closed her eyes and leaned back against the closet door, trying to steady her weak knees. Her body was raging with need for him. She had known that they had chemistry, but what she felt when their lips touched was unlike anything she'd experienced before. She always took things slow with men, always cautious both with her heart and body, but with Evan all she wanted to do was jump in feet first and let the consequences sort themselves out. If the phone hadn't interrupted them she would have eagerly fallen to her knees, pulled down his pants and taken his huge, erect cock in her mouth. She smiled at thought of his come exploding in her waiting mouth.

Opening her eyes, her gaze immediately caught his and she didn't like the look in them - a look of dread.

"Yeah, I'll be right there. Yeah. No problem," he said as he hung up the phone. "Alyssa, I'm sorry."

"The station," she guessed pushing herself off the wall and slowly walking over to him.

He ran a hand through his hair, let out a loud huff and rushed over to his closet to grab his uniform. "Yeah. I'm sorry. Just for a few hours. Why don't you get some sleep and I'll be home to take you shopping when you get up."

Walking over to his bed she flopped herself onto it, and rolled over to her stomach watching him as he crossed the room grabbed a uniform from his closet and began getting dressed. He turned his back to her as he pulled down his bottoms revealing his tight naked ass to her. She groaned inwardly, if it hadn't been for the blasted phone her hands would have been caressing that tight ass right now. In less than a minute he was turning back to face her, fully dressed and looking as sexy as ever, more so now that she knew what was underneath.

"Have I ever mentioned how sexy you are Evan?" she asked grinning.

He returned her grin and shook his head. "Nah, don't believe that you ever did. Pretty sure I'd have remembered you mentioning that." He strode over to her closing the distance between them in several strides.

She rolled to her back at the edge of the bed when he approached and propped herself up on her elbows as he leaned down to her.

"Perhaps we can pick up where we left off when I get home?" he asked ghosting his lips across hers.

"Uh-huh." she murmured as he nipped at her lower lip, taking it between his teeth and sucking gently. Her pussy was throbbing, begging and pleading with her to make him stay. She did her best to ignore it.

Reluctantly, he released her lower lip and kissed her lightly before straightening up again. "Gotta go. Make yourself at home." Without another word he rushed from the room and less than a minute later she heard the front door open and close and then the sound of him starting his Jeep.

Surprisingly enough, the fact that she was technically homeless with literally no possessions was at the back of her mind for the moment. The truth was that her possessions were few and of little value. For a while now she had been considering moving to a better apartment. It was going to be a nuisance buying new things, but luckily she had foresight and had just gotten home insurance. They were simply things that were replaceable in her mind. Evan had told her that everyone in the building had gotten out safely, a couple of people needed to go to the hospital, but all-in-all it hadn't been as bad as it could have been and that was the most important thing.

She groaned loudly as she flopped back down onto the mattress. There was no way in hell she was going to get any sleep in the condition she was in, her pussy throbbing, and her heartbeat racing so quickly that she could feel it thumping against her chest while her head was swimming with thoughts of him.

She could still feel his body against hers and the taste of his lips, taunting her. With a sigh of resignation she knew there was only one way to calm the storm raging inside her, and it happened to be something she'd been doing way too much of lately. She undid the tie on his boxers, loosened the waistband and slipped her hand under the waistband. She spread the soft lips of her pussy wide and began to stroke her clit with two fingers.

"Mmmm Evan," she moaned to the empty room as she imagined that he was laying next to her and it was his hand that was stroking her clit so expertly. She dipped a couple of fingers deep into her drenched core and moaned a little louder as she began to stroke her inner wall in just the right place to bring her close to her breaking point within minutes.

She could feel his body over hers, his thick, long cock pressing against her groin and his tongue teasing the side of her neck. And his scent surrounded her - a spicy musk, reminding her of his closeness. She began to alternate stroking her clit and dipping her fingers deep inside her wet pussy. Faster and harder she stroked herself, bucking against her hand as she came close - so close - to the point of no return.

"Oh God Evan, yes!" she cried out as she bucked harder against her hand. She slipped her other hand under the t-shirt and began pinching her nipple hard. She whimpered as a short shot of pleasure and pain rushed through her.

Close, so close.

She could feel his lips on hers, grazing hers, teasing her just like they had earlier. She parted her lips for him, imagining her tongue slipping past his lips as she caressed the rest of his body.

And then he was there, hovering over her.

She eyes shot open just as his mouth came crashing down on hers and he stretched out beside her onto the bed. Her hand was batted away, from under her borrowed boxers and replaced by his larger, stronger one. She didn't have time to be embarrassed about being caught masturbating in his bed to thoughts of him because as soon as he thrust two fingers deep into her, she cried out as her body tensed up and she exploded over his hand.

"I didn't realize you were planning on starting without me," he teased as her glazed over dark eyes caught his.

She groaned as she closed her eyes and covered her face with her hand. "Oh-my-God. I'm so embarrassed. I just-" She groaned a second time. "You left suddenly, and I was all worked up, and... I just... Oh God."

At the sound of his soft chuckling she uncovered her face and slowly opened her eyes. Cupping her chin in his hand he lowered his mouth to hers and kissed her softly. "Can I share a secret with you?"

"Sure, of course."

"I've thought of you a good number of times over the past few weeks while jacking off. There's nothing to be embarrassed about." He gave her a wickedly sexy grin, displaying the dimples she adored. His smile sent a shiver through her as he took her hand in his and guided it to the front of his pants to his massive erection. "In fact, seeing you like this - while thinking of me - is one of the sexiest things I've seen."

She stroked the ridge of his cock from over the material of his pants. He groaned and closed his eyes for a moment as if savouring the feel of the contact. When he opened them back up his green eyes had turned dark and stormy, filled with his desire.

Alyssa felt another stirring between her legs and once again the fire within her awoke. "Why are you back?"

"Ralph decided to do me a favour and work a double when he found out you were here so I wouldn't have to."

Alyssa began to slowly undo the buttons on his shirt. "That was nice of him."

Evan pushed her flat against the mattress and positioned himself between her legs, holding his weight up with a hand planted at the side of her head. "Very nice," he replied lowering his lips to hers.

With the buttons of his shirt undone, she began to slip it from his shoulders. Pulling his lips from hers and leaving her breathless in the process, he sat back on his heels finished removing the shirt and tossed it to the floor, his undershirt joined it moments later.

Evan began to lower himself once more but she stopped him, sitting up and placing a hand against his chest. "Hold on a second."

Frowning, Evan followed her gaze to his chest and then lower to his stomach. "Alyssa?"

Alyssa reached over and began to trace the hard lines of muscle of his abdominals, the muscle rippled and flexed under her touch. "Amazing," she whispered.

"What?" He looked from her to his stomach and then back again, a slightly confused expression on his handsome features.

Heat rushed to her cheeks. "Your body... It's amazing. So toned. Like you would see on those marble statues of the Greek Gods." Her eyes dipped lower to the massive bulge under his pants and her pussy clenched. Damn, she wanted him.

The sound of his low chuckle brought her eyes back to his as her fingers worked at undoing his belt and then pants.

"I have no idea what to say to that other than thank you, though I think you're overstating slightly." He lowered himself back down, once more pushing her back to the mattress.

His pants now undone, she slipped her hand under his boxers to grasp his thick, hard cock. He groaned as his lips touched the side of her neck. "Fuck, you have no idea how long I've wanted you."

"A month," she teased.

Her teasing was answered by a low growl from the back of his throat. "Smart ass."

His words and tongue as it flicked the sensitive side of her neck had her moaning while sending shivers down her spine. She tightened her grip on his shaft and quickened the speed of her strokes. His cock throbbed in her palm as a small amount of pre-cum seeped from the tip.

His mouth's sweet torment made it as far as her collar, before it came to a grinding halt. "Damned clothing," he growled, grabbing at the bottom of the shirt and pulling it up.

Giggling softly at his enthusiasm Alyssa lifted herself up so he could remove it fully, exposing her bare generous breasts to him.

"Beautiful," he murmured as his head lowered and he sucked her nipple into his mouth. Alyssa gasped as a short flare of pleasure rocked through her as his tongue circled the hardening nipple, and then flicked the tip.

There was still too much clothing remaining between them. Her boxers and his pants seemed too restrictive. She needed to feel his cock slipping between her wet folds, and she needed it worse than she thought she had ever needed anything before.

He nipped her now tight nipple and she whimpered at the short jolt of pleasure pain that rushed through her to pulse between her legs. Releasing his dick momentarily she hooked her thumbs into the band of his pants and pushed them down his hips. With his assistance his pants and boxers fell to the growing pile of clothing on the floor.

Releasing the second nipple, which was now a hardened peak, he looked down their bodies and clucked his tongue off the roof of his mouth as his eyes focused on the only remaining barrier between their bodies, her borrowed boxers.

"It hardly seems fair that you keep an article of clothing after you've stripped me naked," he chided.

She raised a brow at him and smiled wickedly. "Then by all means help yourself."

Alyssa squealed as in one swift movement, Evan grabbed her around the waist and flipped over to his back bringing her with him, while at the same time managing to yank the boxers down and toss them to the floor with the rest of their clothing. He then settled her straddling his waist, his hard thick dick peeping from between her legs.

"Happy now?" Alyssa stretched out over him placing a line of kisses along his chest.

"Very," he confirmed. A low grumble sounded from the back of his throat as she reached between them and settled his dick between her moist folds, the head of his dick pressing against her clit.

Grabbing her ass with both hands, he pulled her down tighter to him making her sigh and grip tight to his broad shoulders in an attempt to calm herself. He hadn't even penetrated her, but she was feeling her body building towards another orgasm simply from the anticipation. She rubbed against him, his cock moving back and forth along her slit, eager to plunge deep into her heated core.

"My God, I want you so badly." She looked up into his emerald green hunger-filled eyes. A part of her wanted to wait until they'd gone on an "official" date and do things properly with him; she didn't want to risk their friendship and possibly more for one night of sex. But the stronger part of her - the part that had been longing for him for weeks now - needed him, needed him to fill her to the hilt and make her come over and over until she collapsed with exhaustion.

He slid a hand up the length of her and then threaded his fingers into her hair. "I think it's my turn to tell you that if you want it, then take it."

She moved against him, flattening her body over hers and kissing her way up his neck, losing herself in the smell of his aftershave and the feel of his warm, hard body under hers. The tip of his cock found its way to her drenched opening, all she needed to do to relieve the tension was pressed down onto him.

Alyssa pulled up slightly from him, her eyes catching his once more and their mouths a fraction of an inch apart, their breaths intermingling. She fisted the blanket on either side of his head, trying to calm herself. Trying to regain control, but it was a futile effort.

She. Needed. Him.

With a quick swift movement she pressed down on him. His cock pushed past her tight opening, stretching her to her limits as it was driven in. She cried out and claimed his lips, as she once more attempted - without success - to steady herself. Her body was a coil that would at any moment break and she needed that release.

She pulled up and slammed back down on him. He groaned against her mouth with a hand in her hair fisting the long, dark locks roughly and his other hand on her ass assisting in pulling her down harder.

Pulling her lips from his she began moving faster, burying her face against her neck as she pulled up and slammed back down onto his hard cock, savouring the delicious shivers that each thrust caused to rush through her. She was so close her stomach pained. Up and down on his shaft, faster and harder, moaning and whimpering as the head of his cock stroked her g-spot.

"Oh fuck honey, let go," he urged, his voice soft and sensual in her ear. "You feel amazing around my cock."

She wanted to. She was going to. Seconds away. And then finally, she screamed out, her screams muffled against his neck as she slammed down onto him, burying him to the balls inside of her warm pussy.

Evan also groaned as her pussy trembled around his cock and her juices rushed down the length of his shaft. Without warning Evan grabbed her and was flipping her onto her back, Sitting up on his knees he hooked one of her legs with his arm, opening her wide to him. Pulled out, until the head of his cock was nearly out, he then slammed back into her.

Alyssa cried out at the sudden forceful impact of his invading cock and the surge of pleasure that came with it.

"So tight. God, you feel unbelievable." He pulled out and slammed back in over and over again. She lifted her head and watched as his long length would appear and then disappear deep within her; she'd never seen anything so arousing. Her eyes became fixated on his cock as it disappeared and reappeared into her smooth shaven pussy. Although she'd already had two orgasms her body was rushing towards yet another.

He increased the speed and force of each thrust and she felt his cock hardening, preparing to explode any moment. Slipping her hand between her legs, she exposed her swollen clit and began rolling it between her fingers bringing herself rapidly towards her third orgasm of the evening.

Looking up, her eyes caught his just as he thrust hard into her a final time and groaned his release. His cum filled her, in several forceful spurts sending her over the edge - yet again. She cried out as her pussy clenched around his cock - milking it. Her body tensed and she exploded over him, her juices mixing with his as he collapsed over her, taking care to brace his fall with a hand at the side of her head to keep from crushing her under his weight.

Evan sighed loudly, his lips brushing hers. "That was incredible Alyssa."

"I know."

Evan stayed buried within her for several minutes, both of them savouring the feel of the other. He slowly slid his depleted shaft from her and their mixture of fluids game rushing out with it. Collapsing to his back, he pulled her over to him. Snuggling up to his side, she placed a kiss on his shoulder and looked up to meet his gaze.

His expression suddenly darkened and his brow furrowed. "Not to ruin the mood or anything, but you did mention the other day about..." He grimaced as if trying to figure a tactful way of putting his thoughts into words. "You had to see the doctor for your, well... you know, your birth control injection. Right?"

Laughing, Alyssa folded her arms across his chest, placed her chin on her arm and peered up at him. "You're just thinking about that now?"

Evan huffed as his face flushed. "Well, see. I came back and you were on the bed, moaning my name. And then we were naked. And before I knew it I was inside of you, and damn, it's been a long while since I've been with someone and you felt, so good. And I'd been hoping for this for as long as I've known you. And..."

Still laughing, Alyssa leaned over him and kissed him quickly. "You were right. It's taken care of, so no need to panic."

"Just so you know I am never, ever careless like that-"

"Evan," she cut in.

"Yeah."

She wrapped her arms around his torso and snuggled close to him and closing her eyes, taking comfort in his embrace. "You can stop talking now."

Chuckling softly, he kissed her temple and pulled her tighter to him as she fell into a satisfied sleep.

Chapter 4

"And what about this one?"

Evan glanced up from the game he was fiddling with on his Smartphone and watched as Alyssa strode out of the dressing room wearing a silver strapless gown. The neckline plunged dangerously low between her breasts, not that he minded. Not in the least. Though he did find himself wondering how it managed to stay covering her amble breasts. The flowing skirt fell just below the knee.

What Evan had thought would be a brief shopping trip for some essential clothing for her had turned into a day long event. This was their final stop, to pick out a dress so she could accompany him to the ball. She wanted him to be there to assist in picking out the dress though he highly doubted his opinion mattered much. In his experience with women, they wanted what they wanted and it was futile to try and change their minds. It was always in the man's best interest to nod and agree with whatever opinions they had about said article of clothing.

She twirled towards him, the skirt fanning out around her and his breath hitched. He felt a stirring within his pants at the sight of the skimpy black thong she wore underneath was revealed a little. Coming to a stop in front of him, her eyes took on a mischievous look as she glanced around the small boutique. The cashier was busy with a customer at the front of the store and there was currently only one other customer browsing.

Striking a pose, her hip thrust out, her hands holding her dark hair bundled up on top of her head she eyed him. "What do you think?"

This was the eighth dress that she's tried on, but this one was easily his favourite of the bunch. The dress looked stunning on her. The bodice gripped her breasts beautifully, teasing his eyes, by revealing just enough to make him crave to see more.

She leaned over him, bracing her hands on the armrests on either side of him. Glancing down he was rewarded with a perfect view of her breasts constrained within the bodice of the dress. Nibbling at her lower lip she caught his gaze. "'I want you."

Evan's cock jerked as he frowned and looked around them once more. "Now?"

Slipped a hand between his legs she stroked the ridge of his growing cock through his jeans. "Now," she confirmed ghosting her lips across his before straightening back up and grabbing his hand, giving it a quick, forceful tug.

Giving in, Evan rose from his chair, tucking the phone into the inner pocket of his leather jacket and with one last look around to ensure no one was watching he quickly followed her into the dressing room. Sex in a dressing room stall, cliché perhaps, but that didn't concern him. As he locked the door to the tiny room, barely large enough to fit the two of them.

As soon as he turned back around, she closed the distance between them, and was pressing her body against him, melting into him. Her breasts crushed against his hard chest and threatened to spill from the bodice as her lips found his, her kiss hungry - demanding.

Groaning, Evan slid his arms around her, and cupped her ass cheeks in his hands, pulling her tight against him, the ridge of his cock pressing against her stomach.

As she kissed him, her hands frantically undid his jeans. Once undone, she hooked her thumbs into the waistband of the pants and tugged them - along with his boxers - down, exposing his erect cock to her. She dropped to her knees in front of him, grasped his dick in her hand and looked up, catching his eyes.

A groan escaped Evan, as he watched her tongue flick the head of his cock, cleaning the pre-cum that was seeping from the slit. He fell back against the door and then threaded his hands into her hair, grasping her head and urging her mouth down on him.

Just a minute or two, he told himself as his hunger filled eyes caught sight of the small blue chair a couple of feet away. He's enjoy a couple of minutes of her sweet mouth wrapped around him before turning her around, bending her over the chair and fucking her from behind.

Her mouth took him in, and she moaned around his cock, the sound of her moan sending sweet vibrations through him. His fingers tightened in her hair and he thrust his hips towards her mouth, prompting her to take in more of his long length. She moaned a second time, ending his temporary torment and taking him in as far as she could, the tip of his cock pressing against the back of his throat. She couldn't manage his full length, but with her hand pumping the base of his dick it didn't matter.

"Dammit, Alyssa. That's good."

She looked up, and caught his eyes.

Looking down he became transfixed watching her as her head bobbed up and down, the length of his shaft, disappearing and reappearing between her glossed lips. Reaching into his pants, she cupped his balls with her free hand. His breath caught in his throat, and he closed his eyes enjoying her gentle caress in combination with her mouth's sucking.

The fire within him increased and he found himself coming closer, so he began to thrust harder into her mouth. She was no longer in control as he began to drive his thick, rigid shaft deep into her throat.

"So. Fucking. Good." Each word was emphasised with a thrust that rammed against the back of her throat and had her gagging slightly, but he found himself having a hard time controlling himself. She had him to excited, too close to losing control. He'd envisioned those lips on his cock so many times over the past few weeks that it seemed almost surreal for it to be happening now, in the dressing room of a bridal and formal wear boutique.

"Stop!" he ordered as he pulled himself out completely. "Bend over that chair," he ordered nodded towards the chair. Flashing him a smile she turned and did as told, lifting her skirt to reveal her firm round ass, she placed a knee on the chair and braced herself with one foot on the floor, gripping the back in her hands.

Looking over her shoulder her dark eyes caught his, "What are you waiting for?"

A soft chuckle left his lips as he took a couple steps and positioned himself behind her. Knowing they were on a limited timetable, he hooked the black string of her thong that was nestled between her wet folds with his index finger and pulled it aside. He ran a finger along her slit, and was rewarded by a soft moan as she moved back against him.

"Please Evan. Now!" she pleaded with him, desperation in her voice.

Evan chuckled at her enthusiasm. He would have loved to spend a little while teasing her, he wanted to hear her *really* beg him. However, a couple of female voices were beginning to come closer the back of the store and they were seriously running low on time.

"Evan!"

He cringed as he positioned his shaft at her entrance and leaned over her. "Be quiet or I stop," he threatened a grin on his lips.

"Yes, Sir," she moaned, pressing back against him attempting to impale herself on his length. Not able to hold back any longer from sinking deep into her moist, trembling pussy he slammed into her and she cried out.

Shit! He leaned over her once more, covering her mouth with his hand. "Damn Alyssa," while his tone was meant to be chastising it came out thick and dripping with his desire. He pulled out and slammed back into her. She moaned out again, but this time his hand stifled much of the sound as her fingers tightening on the back of the chair. Slowly out and once more back in. Her pussy tightened around him. She felt like heaven, her tight dripping wet cunt wrapped tightly around his length.

Two more thrusts and there came a knock at the dressing room door. "Miss, is everything okay in there?"

Evan froze, his cock buried deep inside of her. "You okay to answer," he whispered.

She trembled under him as she nodded.

Not convienced that she could, but knowing he had no choice he removed his hand from her mouth and hoped for the best.

"I'm fine..." she called out, impressing him that she was able to maintain a steady tone in her reply. "I'm almost finished."

There was a moment of silence.

"If you need anything, Miss, then just let me know."

Alyssa giggled softly, looking over her shoulder at him, and then moaned as he pulled out and slammed back into her.

"How did I let you talk me into this?"

She giggled a little louder, "It wasn't that hard."

Grabbing her hips in his hands he pulled out and slammed back in. Again and again, Alyssa bucked back against him, meeting his every thrust. With each thrust he found himself coming closer to the brink. He leaned forward again, his mouth against her ear and his hand reaching around her, parting her pussy lips and exposing her clit. "Are you going to come for me Alyssa?"

"Soon," she whimpered her response as he reached around her, parted her pussy lips and began to stroke her clit as he rammed over and over into her, pulling out almost completely and then driving hard back in.

She had just gotten the word uttered from her lips when she moaned loudly - too loudly - tensed up and then exploded over his cock, covering his thick shaft with her sweet nectar.

That was the final straw for him. Her pussy begged him to give in and let go. Holding tight to her hips he groaned loudly, rammed in hard one final time and a surge of his cum came rushing from him, violently slamming into her moist core, filling her completely and mixing with her own juices.

Evan had to reach out and support himself with a hand on the wall on either side of them as an overwhelming sense of relieve washed over him. "My God Alyssa, you make me crazy," he managed to growl as he regained his composure and slowly, regretfully, pulled himself from her wet heat. A mixture of their juices quickly followed slowly making their way down her inner thighs.

As he pulled up his pants and began to close them back up, while attempting to assist Alyssa out of the dress, the sound of voices outside of the dressing room had both he and Alyssa sharing an alarmed look.

They heard us? Alyssa mouthed over to him.

Ahhh, shit. He shrugged and then ran a hand through his hair. Evan eyed the door which he was thankful went to the floor, keeping the sight of two sets of feet hidden.

A knock sounded at the door. "Miss, would you please step out of the dressing room for a moment." The politeness in her saleswoman's tone was gone. She knew.

Evan wagged a finger at her, scowling.

"S-sure. I-I'll be right out," she squeaked as she finished getting dressed and began to gather the several dressed she'd tried on into her arms.

Evan could feel the heat rushing to his face at the thought of facing the middle-aged sales person as he and Alyssa took the walk of shame through the store. Looking down at Alyssa as she straightened and smoothed down her hair, he was slightly annoyed to see that she had already regained her composure and was beaming up at him. She was supposed to be the shy one dammit!

"So we're taking the silver one?" she whispered stepping up to him quickly and kissing him.

He growled low and nodded. "Let's get this over with." Placing a palm at the small of her back he gave her a slight push forward urging her to open the door.

"Why do I have to go first?" she grumbled, unlocking the door slowly.

"Ladies first," he retorted smirking and pushing the door open wide with his palm revealing the scowling saleswoman, and a couple of customers staring in their direction.

"This is a bridal shop, not a brothel," the sales woman spat as she glared at Alyssa, up to him and back down to her.

"It's not what you think," Alyssa looked up at him and Evan shrugged.

"Please leave my store." She looked from one to the other once more. "Both of you, before I call the police."

The police was the last thing Evan wanted. The crap he'd get from his captain if he got arrested wasn't something he was too eager to experience.

Alyssa looked up at Evan once more then to her silver dress and then to the glowering saleslady. "We're really sorry," she caught her lower lip between her teeth looked up at Evan then back to the sales lady, giving her the most apologetic smile she could muster as she passed her the silver dress, "but could we buy the dress first?"

****

Alyssa sighed and closed her eyes as she took a long, hard gulp from her chocolate milkshake and looked across the cafe table at Evan. Why in the name of God did she convince Evan to fuck her in the dressing room? She could still feel the heat rising to her cheeks each time she thought of it and that had happened close to two hours ago.

She normally wouldn't have been so brazen, but there was something about him. The spark had always been there, but after last night, it was a raging inferno within her that didn't seem to want to simmer. She could easily spend the next few days, hell week, doing nothing but fucking him.

"I'm really sorry about the whole..." she groaned inwardly a she felt her cheeks grow warm - again.

Evan leaned back in his chair, crossing his arms over his thick chest amusement gleaming in his emerald green eyes. "Not to worry.

Wasn't the first time I've been caught with my pants down," when her brow creased he gave her a cocky grin, "so to speak."

Trying to keep her expression stern, Alyssa narrowed her eyes at him. "So when and with who?"

He waved a dismissive hand at her. "Not important."

"No, you just can't bring something like that up and drop it. Come on, spill it."

Her rolled his eyes and huffed, as though he were being forced to give information he treasured. Somehow Alyssa doubted it. He was baiting her.

"Well," she prompted, not being able to keep the curiosity and excitement from her eyes and tone of voice.

"Alright fine. The first time was when I was sixteen. In the girls' locker room at my high school with Misty Ambers. Principal Peterson heard the commotion and she came storming in. I was suspended for two weeks."

Alyssa's face broke out into a grin. "Couldn't you have waited until after school."

"It's evident, my sweet Alyssa, that you haven't a grasp on the extent of the male hormones at age sixteen. I would have done it in the middle of the football field with the school cheering me on if I could have found a female willing."

Alyssa snorted, rolled up a paper napkin and tossed it at him. Hitting him square in the chest, which sent him into a round of laughter. "That's just nasty Evan. Nasty." But she couldn't help but grin as she caught his eyes. With his looks, charm and charisma she imagined he would have had his choice of young women when he was younger.

Evan spread his hands out, palms up. "I told you not to ask."

"But you said the first time." She sat back in her hair and tapped her fingernail against her teeth. "Did your last girlfriend like to do it in public places?" As soon as the question came out of her mouth she wished she could retract it. His smile faded and a vein in the side of his neck flexed as his jaw clenched. "I'm sorry, I didn't mean to..."

With a shake of his head he seemed to shake the dark cloud hovering over his mood and he smiled over at her although his eyes failed to meet hers. "It's not a huge deal. More of a hurt to the ego than anything. The past couple of girlfriends preferred sex with men other than me."

Alyssa's mouth dropped open and then she snapped it back shut. "I'm sorry. I never..."

Standing he gathered their shopping bags in one hand and extended his free hand to her. "Come on. Let's head home."

Accepting his extended hand, Alyssa stood, her eyes scanning him from head to toe. She couldn't imagine ever wanting another man when someone like Evan was around. The idea seemed ludicrous to her. Granted she'd only known him for a month, but she felt that in that month she learned the most valuable of information. He was kind, funny, sexy as hell... As far as the sex was concerned... So far it was mind blowing - for her anyhow. She suspected the feeling was mutual.

Assumingly seeing her perturbed expression Evan brought her hand to his lips, flipped it over and kissed the palm. "I admit that due to experiences with past relationships, *trust* is a very big issue with me, but that's my problem... Not yours." He gave her hand a little tug. "Now let's get home. There is some lingerie I am eager to see you model for me."

Chapter 5

Evan had become somewhat solemn while they drove home since their little discussion on past girlfriends and his problems with trust. The tone in which he said trust was a big issue felt like it had been a warning, even though he covered it quickly by stating it was his problem not hers. Alyssa was desperate to figure a way to pull him out of his mood and the very thing she needed to do it was fast approaching.

"Pull in here!" Alyssa wagged her finger at the parking lot on her side of the road that led to the kinky sex adult toy store. She wasn't one for toys, but she'd been in an adult store with boyfriends in the past and in her experience nothing lightened a mood like a trip to the adult store.

"The sex shop?" Evan raised a questioning brow at her, shrugged, signalled and then turned in where instructed.

"Thirty years old and you've never been in one before?" she met his questioning brow with one of her own.

"Well, yeah, but..." he grinned as he slid the car into an empty spot in front of the building. "You just never stop surprising me."

"Isn't that a good thing?" she teased her hand already on the door handle and opening it up eager to get inside to explore.

Evan chuckled lightly as he caught her eye. "Yeah, I think it is," he decided as he followed her into the neon lit building.

Being that it was midday the large novelty store had only a couple of shoppers, both of them women who were giggling and chattering in hushed voices in front of the vibrators. The sales clerk was an attractive female, light blonde hair with massive breasts who appeared to be roughly Alyssa's age.

"A basket? Is that necessary? How many things are you planning on buying?" Evan teased as she grabbed a red plastic hand basket by the door.

Looking over at him Alyssa didn't reply, but gave him a coy grin, took his hand and led him off to their first stop. The oils and lubes. Standing in front of the wall carrying that carried a massive variety of lubes with varied in function, colour, smell and taste, Alyssa assessed her choices.

Alyssa jumped slightly when Evan stepped behind her, wrapped his arms around her waist and pulled her ass up tight against the hardening ridge of his cock. He nuzzled her neck for a moment, igniting her need for him. "You know, I'm not sure what we'd be needing lube for considering how wet you tend to get for me," his deep, sultry voice washed over her sending a tremor through her that ended with a pulsing between her legs.

She moaned softly and leaned back against him. "Well, you never know when it may come in handy," she managed to whisper. Grabbing a tube of strawberry flavoured she held it up for his inspection. "Strawberry flavoured."

"Oh, I think you taste fine as you are," he countered, his tone now teasing.

She tossed the strawberry lube in the basket and then grabbed some warming and a couple other tubes without really paying much attention to what they claimed to do. Her focus was too trained on the hard body behind her.

He suddenly backed away from her, leaving her stumbling backwards. "Well, if you're really serious about stocking up then we might find these useful." He grabbed a pair of handcuffs covered in black fur from a rack behind them and tossed them into her basket with the lube.

Huh? Alyssa blinked and gave her head a little shake clearing the thoughts of how good he felt in her at the bridal shop earlier that day. Damn, why did he have to work her up like that? Revenge for the bridal shop she imagined.

He grabbed a matching fur flogger and tossed that in along with the handcuffs. He caught her eyes and then pointed to the flogger. "*That* sweetheart is going to be fun to try on you." Next he tossed in a black satin blindfold.

She watched as his eyes landed on the wall of vibrators. The women had moved to the pornographic video section of the store so he grabbed her hand and led her over to them.

"You know Evan, we don't need to go too overboard."

He grinned at her as his eyes ran up and down the length of her body, making her both slightly self-conscious and highly aroused at the same time. He grabbed a medium sized purple vibrator from the wall. "Purple, pink or blue?"

"Blue?"

Putting the purple one back on the wall, he grabbed the blue one. "Good choice. Says they use an innovative ribbing design for *your* pleasure." He gave her a lopsided smile as he pointed to the front of the package, making her giggle. The blue vibrator joined the growing collection of toys.

Not being able to resist herself she set the basket on the floor, slipped her arms around his neck, stretched along the length of his body and kissed him quickly on the lips. "Who'd have thought shopping with you could be so much fun."

"Oh, I think using the purchases will be much more pleasurable," he responded, lowering his lips to capture hers once more.

****

Despite having picked out the outfit with him less than an hour prior, Alyssa was still feeling self-conscious as she assessed her reflection in the bathroom mirror. Evan had picked out a black and white striped prisoner costume for her to wear for him. He thought it would work well with the handcuffs he'd bought for them. The skirt was so short that if she bent, even slightly she'd be exposing her naked pussy to the world. The top was skin tight and buttoned down the front and dipped low into her cleavage, while pushing her breasts up and together. The worst of it was the boots. The boots were thigh high with a stiletto heel so high that she feared she'd trip and make a complete fool of herself on her way to the bed.

Removing the clip that was holding her hair into a loose bun at the top of her head she let her long dark silken locks cascade down her back. *There's nothing to be shy about, he's been you're closest friend for a month now and he wants you!* She reminded herself, trying to gather the courage to face him.

Taking a deep breath in, she grabbed the door handle, pulled it open and stepped out into the bedroom. Her eyes immediately went to the bed, where Evan was reclined wearing only his jeans, his hands laced behind his head watching the news on the television mounted on the opposite wall. Upon realizing she's entered the room he immediately turned off the television and tossed the remote onto the night table by the bed.

His eyes widened and he licked his lips. He then whistled his appreciation as his eyes slowly made their way down the length of her and then back up to meet her eyes. The intensity in his stare took her breath away momentarily and ignited the fire between her legs. He cleared his throat and raked a hand through his hair as he sat up on the bed. "You look... so fucking sexy Alyssa. Beautiful."

She cocked her head and gave him a wink. "So, glad we made that last stop before coming home?"

"Oh, hell yeah," he confirmed as he slid from the bed and slowly stalked towards her.

She chewed at her lower lip, watching him in anticipation of what he had planned for her. The assortment of toys they'd purchased were lined up on the night table waiting to be used. She didn't have much time ponder it. When he reached her, he pushed her against the wall with his hard body, and his lips claimed hers roughly.

She gasped at his enthusiasm and he took it as an invitation to slip his tongue between her lips. With a moan she slid her hands up his hard, finely contoured muscular chest and laced them behind his neck, pressing herself against him. His cock, already rock solid pressed against her stomach, making her yearn to free it from his jeans, fall to her knees and take him into her mouth.

But this was his fantasy, so she was at the mercy of what he wanted from her. Another shiver rushed through her thinking of the possibilities.

"Mmmm," he moaned pulling his lips from hers and stepping back and looking down at her, his green eyes examining each and every inch of her.

"So now what do you plan on doing with me?" She took a step forward and closed the distance between them.

He didn't answer, but spun her around and walked her backwards towards the bed until the back of her legs hit the bed. "I think my little prisoner needs to be taught a lesson."

Raising an inquisitive brow at him she grinned. "What kind of lesson?" Although she asked she knew full well that whatever he had planned for her it would involve the pair of handcuffs. They seemed to have been his favourite item, besides the outfit, that they'd picked up at the store.

He gave her a devilish grin, swooped down, grabbed her upper thighs and tossed her onto the bed. She giggled as she landed, spread-eagled on the bed. Her skirt had inched up just enough that he could see she was without panties. His lust filled eyes were immediately directed to the apex between her legs and a soft growl came from him.

As suspected, Evan grabbed the handcuffs, leaned over her and quickly cuffed her first wrist. Looping the chain around one of the rungs on the headboard above her head, then he grabbed her free wrist and secured it as well. Once done, he stood and shed his jeans and boxers. He was now standing naked, his big beautiful cock fully erect with a drip of pre-cum escaping from the tip.

Unconsciously, Alyssa swiped her tongue across her lower lip as her eyes wandered over his muscular body. Pure perfection if she'd ever seen it. She wanted to touch him - badly. She pulled at the cuffs, knowing she couldn't free herself, but not being able to keep herself from at least trying.

Evan chuckled as he leaned over and placed a chaste kiss on her lips. He slipped onto the bed and stretched out alongside her. "So what am I going to do with you?" he asked, more to himself than to her as he trailed his index finger along her collarbone and down along the valley between her breasts.

She shook her head, her eyes locked to his. The pulsing between her legs intensified and she squirmed trying to relieve the building pressure.

He unbuttoned the first button on her top, then the second and third. When the forth came loose, the spandex material parted exposing her lush naked breasts to him. Leaning over her he took the nipple closest to him in his mouth. A short rush of pleasure raced through her and she moaned softly.

His tongue circled the large beige nipple turning it into a hardened peak, while his hand palmed the other, his fingers pinching and rolling the nipple.

"Evan," she gasped, squirming and pulling at her restraints. God, she wanted him and she *needed* relief soon. His rock solid cock pressed against her hip teasing her.

He chuckled and began to slowly move down the length of her body. His soft kisses teasing the sensitive flesh of her stomach and moving lower. She began to gently buck against his mouth as his lips came to the waistband of her skirt.

Looking up, his eyes took on a mischievous gleam as they caught hers. "I don't think you'll need this anymore." Hooking his thumbs into the waistband of the skirt he slowly slid it down over her hips. His mouth hovered over her pussy, the warmth of his breath becoming nearly unbearable.

She wiggled under him, once more testing the strength of the cuffs. "Please Evan!"

He glanced back up at her, a sexy smirk touching his lips and he continued his torment, his lips ghosting across the skin of her inner thigh as he pulled the material down further. "I think we'll keep the boots on. Love the boots," he muttered, though she wasn't sure if he was informing her or just speaking out loud to himself.

Sitting up, he slipped the skirt all of the way off and tossed it to the floor.

"I need you Evan," Alyssa gasped, her voice breaking.

He leaned over and kissed her lightly on the lips once more. "It was your idea to go to the sex store," he reminded her and she groaned at the reminded.

"Please." She caught her lower lip between her teeth.

He glanced over at the night table and then down at her smooth shaven pussy. "Spread your legs."

She nodded and eagerly spread her legs, hoping he'd have it in his heart to relieve her of the torture she was enduring.

Evan settled himself between her legs, his eyes now focused intently on her exposed dripping wet, pink pussy. Alyssa whimpered as he slipped his index finger along the length of her slit, from her anus to her clit. The anticipation had gotten her to the point where she was on the edge and only a small push away from exploding.

Leaning over her, he traced her lower lip with his finger coated in her juices. She moaned as she sucked his finger into her mouth licking it clean of her nectar.

His breath caught in his throat for a moment. "Fuck Alyssa," he finally managed to groan.

Alyssa caught his gaze, noticing her own desire reflected in his eyes and smiled softly, loving the fact his teasing was almost as tormenting to him as it was to her. "I need you Evan."

He kissed her once more on the lips, before travelling back down her torso to position his head between her legs. Damn, he looked good down there, his mouth less than an inch from her throbbing core and how she wanted to thread her fingers into his short dark hair and force his mouth into her wet cunt.

"So fucking wet. Love it." He spread her soft folds exposing her swollen clit and drenched pussy and then blew a steady stream of air along her length. Alyssa closed her eyes as she gasped as a wave of pleasure rushed through her, while she struggled with renewed vigour against her restraints. Lowering his head, his mouth gently caressed her clit, flicking the nub with his tongue while thrusting two fingers deep into her moist core.

Alyssa bucked against his hand and mouth as she moaned, her hands fisting above her head. She was painfully close now. Evan pulled his fingers from her and thrust them back in, stroking her inner wall while sucking hard on her clit and that was all she needed.

"Oh my God. Evan Yes. Evan!" she screamed out his name. Her body tensed and then with a rush of relief her pussy exploded in an orgasm so intense that it brought tears to her eyes, covering his hand with her juices as it seeped from her and down her ass.

Removing his fingers from her, he immediately stopped his torment of her clit and buried his face between her legs. He eagerly lapped up every ounce of her juices as though he was a starving man and her pussy juice was the only form of nourishment left in the world. His tongue swept viciously through her pussy, every stroke more intense than the last.

She bucked wildly against his mouth as he began to thrust his tongue in and out of her core - she was thrashing so wildly he settled a hand on her pelvis to secure her to the bed, which only increased her agony. His tongue pistoned in and out as if he were fucking her with his magnificent cock, while he began to explore her ass with his juice coated finger.

"Oh God, fuck me Evan. Please!" she cringed at the needy tone of her voice, but the sweet pleasure he was bringing her was too intense, too much, but at the same time not enough. She was rapidly ascending the summit once more, her body winding so tightly that her stomach was beginning to ache from the need to release.

"Come for me first," he demanded.

His demand was all she needed. She closed her eyes and threw her head back in the pillow, channelling her focus on the sensations that he was bringing about with his tongue. She moaned loudly, while bucking wildly against his mouth and prodding finger as she fell over the summit and exploded. Her eyes were no longer shut and she was panting hard, and feeling slightly light-headed. Her body went limp and she closed her eyes again, this time basking in the aftermath of her second orgasm.

"Good girl."

She hardly noticed him slipping his finger from her ass or him slipping from the bed. Her eyes flew open when she heard the sound of her cuffs being rattled as Evan unlocked the cuffs from her wrists and tossed them to the night table. While tired and sated, she hoped he wasn't finished with her yet, but said nothing. Instead she watched as he examined the table of goodies for a moment before grabbing a bottle of lube.

Catching her eye, he smiled down at her. Though the smile was friendly, the look of heated desire in his eyes sent a shiver through her. "Evan?"

Sitting on the bed next to her he leaned over and kissed her tenderly. He lifted his head slightly so he could peer into her eyes. "Have you ever had someone take that nice tight pussy and your ass at the same time?"

Her eyes widened as she shook her head. "I've been curious about it though," she finally admitted feeling her face flush slightly as though she'd just admitted so something highly scandalous. Again, she wondered how any woman in their right mind would want someone else when they had such a wonderfully beautiful and seductive man like Evan at home.

Evan ghosted his lips across hers. "Will you try it?"

Alyssa moaned softly against his lips. Would she try it? She'd try just about anything for him at that moment. Despite her two orgasms, the familiar tingle between her legs started back up. "Yes," she whispered.

"Flip over honey."

She did as told rolling over to her stomach, then positioned herself onto her hands and knees. She then grabbing a pillow and leaned forward, lowering her chest to the mattress as he grabbed the vibrator, along with the lube and positioned himself behind her on his knees.

"Spread your legs further apart and relax I don't want to hurt you," he said as he flipped open the tube and smeared a generous amount on her. "Have you had anal before?"

"Yes." *But not with a cock as big as yours.* She wanted it, but at the same time she was slightly intimidated by his size. He was big, much bigger than she'd had in the past. Taking a few deep breaths in and releasing them she found herself starting to relax somewhat.

"Many times?" he asked as he spread the warming lube on her. It warmed as he rubbed it onto her, along her slit, with his primary focus being her anus. Placing one hand on the small of her back he slipped one finger into her ass.

"Twice," she gasped from the sudden invasion and instinctively clinched around his probing finger.

"Mmmm. Relax baby," He whispered, soothing and relaxing her. Sliding the hand that was on his lower back around her waist he palmed her pussy, spread her pussy lips and began to stroke her swollen clit.

She whimpered and immediately relaxed as the sensations his fingers were bringing to her as they played with her nub increased her need to have him in her. Ass, pussy, mouth, she didn't care at this point as long as he was filling her.

He pumped his single index finger in her ass a few minutes while stroking her clit before adding a second finger and scissoring his fingers, stretching her ass so she could accommodate his girth. "Oh-my-god," She moaned and began to push back against him, needing his fingers in deeper, faster. Alyssa fisted the pillow under her. "Evan. Oh God, I love it. I need it,"

He didn't respond, but seemingly satisfied that she was ready to accommodate him, he pressed the head of his cock to the tight rim of muscle guarding her tight ass. He pressed slowly into her. His cock stretched her ass further than it had ever been stretched causing an intense burning making her cry out against the pillow.

"Relax honey," he whispered as he began to work her clit again, pinching hard and rolling the quivering nub between his fingers.

She took another breath in and let her body relax under his expert touch. When he felt she was relaxed enough he continued pressing. "Damn, so tight. You feel amazing baby."

She could only moan and whimper. The burning pain was gone and now replaced by the need to have his huge shaft in deeper. She bucked back against him and he groaned.

"Easy," he advised.

"I need you. It's okay."

He groaned and then chuckled as she bucked back against him again. "It's me, not you. Feels so fucking good that you're going to be making me cum before I have a chance to insert the vibrator."

Loving the affect she was having on him, Alyssa looked back over her shoulder at him, gave him a wicked grin and wink and then bucked back against him once more. He closed his eyes and groaned, his hands now on her hips gripping them tightly.

"Damn, Alyssa," he opened his eyes and they caught hers. A rush of electricity raced through her as their eyes locked. He returned her smile and grasping her hips tightly, rammed his cock into her ass, balls deep. She moaned loudly, her chest falling back onto the pillow once more.

Moments later, with his cock still buried deep into her, tormenting her with its presence, she heard the faint buzz of the vibrator and the coolness which quickly turned to warmth as he spread some more lubricant between her soft, moist folds.

"I'm not wet enough already," she teased, though considering she could feel her juices slowly sliding down her inner thighs she knew she was.

Without answering her, he placed the tip of the thick vibrating toy at her opening and slid it into her. She moaned loudly as it the combination of his cock in her ass and vibrator in her pussy had her feeling fuller than she'd ever experienced before and sent her nearly over the edge. When the vibrator was fully inserted, massaging her inner wall and sending wave after wave of pleasure through her, Evan began to move within her tight ass.

"I'm coming." she cried out as she crested the summit, yet again. Her body tensed, she fisted the pillow, her pussy clenched, and then she released a rush of her fluids. But this time she was not allowed the luxury of basking in her aftermath of her release as Evan began to pound into her ass mercilessly, a soft grunt accompanying each thrust.

"That's it, come for me. Over and over." he groaned jack-hammering into her ass. And Alyssa obliged, she found herself taken through a series of orgasms one after another in rapid succession.

She clawed at the sheets below her, as she bucked wildly against him meeting each of his thrusts.

Just when she thought she couldn't handle another moment of the sweet pleasure he was producing within her, his hands tightened on her hips. His fingers dug, almost painfully, into the flesh and he groaned loudly, thrusting one final time so hard that he sent her falling forward onto her stomach on the bed as he released. Spurt after spurt spewed violently into her ass as he unloaded in what seemed like a never ending series of climaxes.

When he was finished releasing into her, he slowly withdrew his cock and then the vibrator quickly after, leaving her sated, but at the same time feeling very empty. She rolled over to her back and watched as he deposited the condom he'd put on sometime before entering her ass, though she had never realized he'd even done it and placed the vibrator next to the rest of the toys on the night table.

Slipping back into bed, he pulled her against his side and kissed her temple. "I assume you enjoyed it?"

She giggled as she placed a chaste kiss on his chest and then looked up to meet his eyes. "You are the most amazing, beautiful, and surprising person I've ever met."

Evan grinned giving her a tight squeeze. "Considering how sore I suspect you'll be in the morning, I have a feeling you may change your mind on that."

"Mmmm, we'll see." Exhausted, she laid her head back down on his chest and dozed off into a deep sleep.

Chapter 6

The past couple of days had been a dream for Alyssa. Being with Evan was better than she could have imagined it could or would be. He was easily the kind of man that a woman could fall head over heels for, at a rapid pace. The sex was the most incredible she'd ever experienced and as they became more familiar with each other sexually, her need for him intensified. She felt like she was sixteen all over again. But this time she was discovering that first special love for a second time and the feeling was divine.

The fact Samantha was seething over the recent development was an added bonus. The look on Samantha's face when she'd told her about her relationship with Evan was so priceless that Alyssa didn't even feel the need to confront her about lying to Evan. There simply seemed to be no point in rocking the boat. It all worked out and that was all that mattered.

"So I'll see you in a few hours."

Alyssa smiled and nodded raking a hand through her long silken locks. "Can't wait."

Planting a hand against the outside wall of the coffee shop at the side of her head, Evan leaned into her capturing her lips with his. She moaned as she fisted the front of his t-shirt and pulled him into her.

Unfortunately for her Samantha was working tonight, and she could feel the other woman's eyes burrowing a hole in the back of her skull as she parted her lips and Evan deepened the kiss, his tongue slipping past her lips and caressing her tongue with his. A series of intense shots of pleasure rushed down her spine and pulsed between her legs. It took all of her strength not to pull him behind the dumpster and make him fuck her then and there. Perhaps it wouldn't have been the most elegant of locales, but at that moment location wasn't an issue.

The sound of a car horn beeping brought her back to reality and she reluctantly loosened her grip on the front of his shirt. "I gotta go start my shift."

He cupped her chin in his hand and gave her a final chaste kiss on the lips. "See you in a couple hours okay?"

She nodded. "Uh-huh."

"Alright." He slowly backed away from her and she immediately felt saddened by the loss of his closeness; she both hated and loved the giddy feeling he invoked within her.

Alyssa watched him as he gave her a final nod, turned and quickly made his way across the street to the station. She fell back against the wall of the restaurant, and exhaled loudly as she continued to watch him walk away.

Taking one more deep breath in and releasing, Alyssa pushed herself off of the wall and made her way into the coffee shop.

"Cut it awful close didn't you?" Samantha called out from the kitchen as Alyssa locked the door behind her and made her way to the drive-thru window.

She somehow doubted Samantha was referring to the start of her shift, but more a jab towards how long it took for her to finally get him, so refused to respond as she pulled her hair up into a bun.

Seemingly annoyed that Alyssa refused to be baited, Samantha came from the kitchen to the drive-thru section. "Bet it would never have happened if he hadn't had to rescue you."

Oh for the love of God. Alyssa closed her eyes and slowly counted backwards from ten. Why did Samantha want to pick a fight? Why Evan? Samantha could have her choice of men, why was she so hellbent on the one man that was Alyssa's? Just as quickly as the question popped into her mind did the answer come rushing with it. Because he was hers, and because he was one of the only men in Portland that didn't want Samantha. It was going to be a long shift with Samantha. *Why did Jenny have to take the day off?*

"You know Samantha, there's been an attraction between us since the first night we met. It would have happened eventually."

Samantha didn't have a chance to voice her rebuttal, because the headset dinged and the voice of the Ass Man came over the headset. For one of the first times since she'd began working at the coffee shop, Alyssa was actually grateful to have him coming through the drive-thru.

****

Alyssa spent most her first couple of hours attempting to avoid Samantha, which was difficult considering they were in such close proximity and needed to work together. But just over two hours into her shift a very familiar voice came over the drive-thru speaker, her most recent ex-boyfriend and slime ball extraordinaire, Kevin.

"Alyssa. Come out I need to see you."

"Kevin?"

He didn't reply but instead drove his car around to the front of the coffee shop and hurried out. He stumbled a couple of times, but eventually made it to the front door and knocked.

Friday night and stumbling out of his car meant one thing. He was drunk and a drunk Kevin was a persistent and annoying one.

"Damn, damn, damn," Alyssa grumbled pulling off her headset. "Samantha, I'm going on a break. I'll be right back."

"Sure." Samantha peeked her head out from the kitchen and glanced over to the front of the store. She took notice of the tall, lanky, blonde-haired man waiting for Alyssa, then turned back to her and grinned. "More than one Alyssa?"

Fuck! "No, it's not like that. He's an ex and he's drunk." Alyssa shook her head and waved a dismissive hand at Samantha. "I'll be right back."

Samantha nodded, her grin widening. "Sure."

Rushing to the door, Alyssa opened it up and slipped out locking it behind her. Taking a quick glance over at the station and then inside the restaurant where Samantha watched while pretending to work, she grabbed his arm and pulled him around the corner of the building so they were out of the line of view from prying eyes. She'd tell Evan about Kevin stopping by later, but knowing Kevin when he was drinking God only knew what he'd do or say so she preferred that they be out of sight and listening range.

"Thank God you're okay!" Kevin pulled her tight into his arms, knocked the wind out of her as his arms tightened around her torso.

"I'm fine." She pushed at his chest, but he refused to budge. She groaned inwardly. "What are you doing here?"

"I found out about the fire. I was worried." He buried his face in her hair, his mouth near her ear and the stench of beer drifted to her nose, making her stomach turn.

"Kevin please." She pushed against him once more, trying to wiggle free. "We haven't been together for a couple of months. Why now? And why are you driving drunk?"

He pulled back slightly, his dazed blue eyes capturing hers. "I've missed you. I didn't realize how much until I thought something may have happened to you."

Closing her eyes briefly she attempted to calm her frazzled nerves. "You should have thought about that before you fucked around on me Kevin."

"I'm so sorry about that Alyssa. Please. Let's try again."

Alyssa's dark eyes widened. Was he for real? What would even give him the idea that she's even *consider* taking him back. She had a sinking suspicion the reason may be inside the coffee shop. There was no way Samantha would stoop so low as to call Kevin, would she? Yeah, she would Alyssa decided, her anger building within her.

"I've moved on. I suggest you do as well."

"I know you still want me. I can tell. Just give it another chance."

She attempted to wiggle away from him once more, but he easily overpowered her pushing her roughly against the wall of the coffee shop as his lips came crashing down onto hers.

****

"I have to hand it to you brother. You went from 0 - 60 pretty quick," Ralph joked as he examined the cards in his hand and waited for Evan to make is play.

Evan shrugged, throwing down two cards. "Sometimes you just need that little shove and then everything falls into place. For the first time in my life I think I may have found *the* one."

"Well, good for you. Consider yourself lucky, I know if I wasn't married I'd..."

Evan chuckled and held up a hand. "Please. Don't finish what you're about to say. That's the girlfriend you're talking about."

Ralph grinned. "Just saying, you're lucky she was still available man."

Glancing up at the clock mounted on the wall of the office Evan noted the time and laid down his cards for Ralph to see. "Full House."

"Well, motherfucker," Ralph tossed down is cards face up on the table. "Two pair. It's past 2am, don't you have somewhere to be?"

Laughing, Evan stood. "Sore loser. I'll be back in a bit."

Ralph waved a dismissive hand at Evan. "Bring me back a coffee and blueberry muffin."

Making his way out of the station, Evan's eyes scanned the inside of the coffee shop, but he couldn't spot Alyssa anywhere, the only person he saw was Samantha manning the drive-thru window. He frowned. Alyssa was usually ready and waiting for him, around this time she'd normally be spying on him while pretending to wipe down tables.

Crossing the street and entering the parking lot he noticed an unfamiliar navy blue car parked in front of the store, with no occupants. Walking up to the side door he knocked onto the window successfully gaining Samantha's attention.

Finishing up with the customer she was serving, she made her way over to him and gave him a wide smile as she unlocked the door and poked her head out. "She's outside talking to some guy."

"Some guy?" Evan echoed as he craned his neck to see the car parked in the parking lot.

"Yeah, I think they're around the corner of the building. They looked pretty chummy."

"You don't say..." his frown deepened and he started to get a bad feeling in the pit of his stomach. "Thanks." Turning from her, Evan quickly made his way around the building until he heard hushed voices.

"I know you still want me..." Evan couldn't make out the rest, but the voice made him pick up the pace until he was around the corner and facing the source of the voices. A tall, blonde man, had his arms wrapped around Alyssa, kissing her passionately.

Anger welled up within Evan. His first instinct was to rush over pull the man from Alyssa and give him a beating he wouldn't soon forget. He took a step forward, but stopped himself, reconsidering. No, he'd been through this situation before and violence wasn't the answer. If she wanted that other man, she could have him. At least he found out the truth now instead of later.

Soundlessly he turned and made his way quickly back to the fire station without taking even a glance back. Yes, this was just another failed relationship to add to his growing list. Problem was despite knowing her for less time than the others it seemed to hurt a hell of a lot more.

****

Several hours later, Alyssa was still frazzled over Kevin showing up and trying to "persuade" her to take him back. She had drunk three glasses of water and a cup of coffee and she still had the taste of him in her mouth. Or maybe it was guilt. She knew she hadn't done anything wrong, she'd managed to push him away and in no uncertain terms told him he would never, ever have a chance with her again. Ever. He'd finally gotten the hint and she'd called him a cab and then called his sister to come pick up his car. But she still felt guilt over it.

It was a busy night, uncharacteristically busy so it wasn't until past 4am that she realized that she hadn't heard nor seen Evan all evening. There hadn't been a fire so it was a slow night, he normally would have been over to visit her a couple of times by now. So where was he?

She rushed back into the kitchen where Samantha was busy glazing donuts, her back turned to Alyssa. "Have you seen Evan at all tonight?"

Samantha froze, her back straightened and she squared her shoulders as if she were preparing for a fight. Peculiar. Slowly she turned and clucked her tongue off of the roof of her mouth. "You know what. Yes. Yes I did. He dropped by earlier."

Alyssa gasped, as if she were punched in the stomach. If he was over then that meant he'd dropped by while she was with Kevin. A sick feeling washed over her. What if...

She wanted to scream at the other woman, but she kept her cool. For some reason Samantha hated her and starting a fight would only add to Samantha's satisfaction and she'd be damned if she was going to do that. "When was he here and what did he say?"

"He showed up when you were with that other guy. Dunno wasn't paying much attention."

Like hell you weren't, you conniving bitch! Alyssa balled her hands into fists, and took a couple of deep breaths in and releasing them. "I'm going on a break. I'll be back in a bit."

Samantha smiled at her sweetly, but the sweetness didn't quite follow through to her eyes which were regarding Alyssa as if she were the enemy. "I hope everything is alright between you two. If you need to talk I'm here for you."

I bet you are! Without another word to Samantha, Alyssa turned on her heel and exited the coffee shop. She had no idea what she was going to say to Evan. She knew he'd been burned in the past so she could only imagine the thoughts that must have raced through his mind when she saw her with Kevin; if he'd seen Kevin kiss her.

Bursting through the front door of the fire station she headed for the break room where the men usually hung out. When she entered all chatter stopped and five sets of eyes focused on her, including Evans. She gulped down the urge to turn and run back to the coffee shop. Did they all know about the kiss? Did they all think she was a liar and a cheat?

"I'll be right back guys," Evan stood and tossed his playing cards onto the table in front of him. His green eyes, vacant of emotion, locked onto hers as he made his way across the room towards her. Grabbing her elbow, he ushered her into one of the offices and closed the door firmly behind them.

"It wasn't what you may think," Alyssa blurted.

Evan sighed, as he crossed the room and perched himself on the edge of the best at the back of the small room. "And what *exactly* do I think? Tell me Alyssa, I'd like to hear what you think I think."

Alyssa eyes him. He didn't appear angry or upset, just indifferent. Like regardless of what she said it wouldn't matter either way. "I didn't invite or want the kiss. He was drunk. He thought he may have had a shot. I don't know." She wanted to go to him, but restrained herself.

"That's funny, because it didn't look like you were anxious for it to end, from where I stood."

"How long *did* watch?"

"Long enough."

"Apparently not long enough to see me push him away. Or hear the conversation before or after the kiss. Or long enough to see me slap him." A sliver of anger developed. Her own hurt over the fact that he'd automatically think the worse, threatened to spill out, but she kept it in check. She had an idea as to his history with women, and she was sure what little he did see, along with Samantha's urging, didn't paint the best picture.

Evan remained silent, his eyes locked to hers, his impassive expression softening. "No I didn't. Who was it Alyssa? And why was he kissing you?"

Encouraged by his softening expression, Alyssa closed the distance between them until she was standing between his legs. "That was Kevin, an old boyfriend. The one just before I met you. He heard about the fire and was concerned so he came looking for me, but he was also drunk and overstepped his boundaries." She sighed and ran her index finger along his jaw. "You're not the only one with fucked up past relationships Evan. I know what it's like to be hurt and betrayed."

They both remained silent for several minutes. Alyssa held her breath as she watched Evan processing the information. *Please let him believe me*, she silently prayed. He was already such an important part of her life that the thought of losing him pained her.

Slipping a hand behind his neck, she pulled his forehead down to her, their breaths intermingling. "I remember you mentioning him. I'm sorry Alyssa. I know I shouldn't assume the worst. I just..."

She ghosted her lips across his. "For the first time in my life I feel like I'm with the man I was meant to be with. Don't you know that?" Alyssa admitted, her voice was barely more than a whisper.

"I know that I've known you for only a month and what I feel for you is stronger than anything I've ever felt for anyone and it scares me."

Alyssa pulled back from him and looked deep into his green eyes and she could see the affection and the fear along with a number of other emotions and she felt her heart suddenly quicken. He was in love with her, it was as plain as day.

She caught her lower lip between her teeth and nibbled nervously. Should she tell him how she felt? Just because he had those feelings towards her didn't mean he was ready to hear them uttered from her lips.

Before she could make up her mind either way, Evan slipped his free hand around her waist and pulled her flush against him. She gasped, and his lips came crashing down onto hers. His tongue forced entry into her mouth as stood and hoisted her up onto his hips. In one swift, powerful movement he twirled her around and lay her down onto the desk, his body covering hers.

Pulling her shirt out from her pants, he slipped a hand under and cupped her breast over the black lace bra. "Maybe I should make sure you forget that little fucker," Evan growled pulling his lips from hers and beginning a string of kisses down the length of her neck.

She moaned softly. "Here? Now?" Not that she objected to doing it on the desk, but the fact that she only had a fifteen minute break crossed her mind momentarily. It was quickly followed by the fact she was working with Samantha and all thoughts of going over her allotted break time were forgotten. Screw Samantha.

To her dismay Evan stopped kissing the side of her neck and pulled his hand from under her shirt. Placing a hand on either side of her head, securing her body against the desk under him he caught her eyes with his hunger filled ones. "I don't want another man to even be a thought in the back of the mind of the woman I love."

"I...Um." Alyssa gulped down the lump forming in her throat, hardly able to believe her own ears. *The woman he loved...* Damn, she loved the sound of that coming from his lips. She touched the side of his face that was just showing the signs of a light morning shadow. "You love?"

"I love," Evan confirmed. "I realize it's quick. But it's how I feel about you.""

A soft smile touched her lips, as she looked up at him in disbelief.

"I think this is the part where you tell me you love me back," he teased before kissing her lightly on the lips.

"I love you Evan." Slipping her arms around his neck, she pulled his lips down to hers, her body on fire with desire for him, needing to feel him filling her. "Do you think the other guys would notice if I show you how much here and now?"

"Think I care if they do?" he murmured as he once more deepened the kiss.

A surge of desire rushed through her and the wetness between her legs increased. She needed him - badly. As her hands frantically undid his pants he worked equally as quick on hers, both of them anxious to feel their bodies joined as one. The thought that there were four men just a room away who could hear what was going on inside the tiny office turned her on rather than shy her away from the idea.

She was the first to finish undoing his pants and pushing them down over his hips and grasping his thick, erect cock in her hand, but she was first only by seconds. He quickly pulled her pants down to her ankles, and then urged her to bend her knees to her chest, doubling her over somewhat uncomfortably, before thrusting two fingers deep into her dripping wet pussy.

"Oh-my-God Evan!" Alyssa closed her eyes and moaned as she grasped the edge of the desk above her head.

Evan leaned over her, his lips grazing the side of her neck, moving upwards until his lips touched her earlobe as his fingered continued to pump her heated core. "I'll make love to you when we get home, but right now I'm going to fuck his hot little pussy of yours, fast and hard, until I feel you come over my cock," he whispered in her ear, his voice thick with his desire and sending a shiver down her spine.

"Tease!" Alyssa opened her eyes to catch his gaze.

He slipped his fingers from her, leaving her whimpering for him to once again fill her. She was not left waiting long. His cock replaced his fingers at the entrance of her needy cunt, pressing into her slowly.

"Evan, please. I need it. Now!" she pleaded, gripping tighter to the edge of the desk and moving against him, urging him to take her.

"I love it when you beg me like that ," without anther word he slammed into her, his cock filling her to the hilt, stretching her to her limits and driving deeper into her than he'd ever been before. She cried out, but his lips came crashing down on hers, muffling the noises coming from her.

Pulling out until his cock was just barely breaching her entrance he slammed into her a second time moving the desk a portion of an inch from the force. Her grip tightened to the edge of the desk as he pulled out of her pussy before slamming his dick into her once more. With each thrust the head of his shaft rubbed against her inner wall, bringing her closer and closer to the brink.

Pulling his lips away from hers, he once more began to work his way down the length of her neck. Turning her head to the side she gasped, both from another powerful thrust, but also because in their distraction they'd forgotten to ensure that the window blinds were closed. The blinds were open and they were perfectly visible to anyone who was inclined to look and at that moment it was Samantha who stood on the dining room pretending to clean off the tables, but in fact was watching her co-worker get fucked on a desk in the fire station.

Her immediate impulse was to stop Evan and quickly get dressed, but his lips against the tender flesh of her neck and the feel of him bringing her closer and closer to the point of no return. His momentum had increased and she was now enjoying the deviant satisfaction she was getting from knowing Samantha was watching

"Oh, God. Harder. I need it Evan!" In the back of her mind she knew she should tell Evan that they were being watched, but she didn't. Instead she bucked harder against him, moaning louder, losing herself in the sensations his massive cock was bringing forth within her.

"Shhh. Do I have to gag you woman," he chided.

"Yes!" Letting go of the edge of the desk, she wrapped her arms around his waist and held tight to him as she was overtaken by an explosive climax. Her pussy tightened around his cock, coating it with her juices and begging him to come with her.

"Yes!" he confirmed, burying his face into her hair and driving deep into her a final time and then joining her as he released deep within her heated core.

She clung to him for a moment savouring the feel of his hard body over hers.

"Alyssa?"

"Yes," she opened her eyes and looked up to see him frowning.

"I think Samantha was watching us..."

A guilty smile touched her lips.

His mouth dropped in disbelief as he slowly pulled out of her, took her hand and pulled her up from the desk and to her feet. "Was she watching the whole time? And why in the name of God didn't you tell me?" Quickly he did up his pants and helped her with hers.

"I got caught up in the moment," she offered.

He huffed and shook his head at her. "What am I going to do with you woman?"

She slipped her arms around his neck and grinned up at him. Feeling brazen she replied teasingly, "spend the rest of your life making me happy?"

With a sigh he drew her into his arms and smiled down at her. "Hmmm. Now that's a simply irresistible offer my darling...."

When he lowered his lips to hers once more, she melted into him and was grateful that this time, it was she, Alyssa Thornton, who found the man of her dreams at the coffee shop.

The End

Soft & Hard Erotic Publishing
www.elixaeverett.com

Contact Information

Website: www.elixaeverett.com
Email: terry.towers@hotmail.ca
Facebook: Terry Towers
Twitter: TerryTowersXXX

Works By Terry Towers

Available Now - Singles
Frat Party Partner Swap
Under the Officer's Command
Daddy's Special Christmas Gift
All For Daddy (Taboo Edition)
The Marine's Naughty Sister (Taboo Edition)
Little Virgin Sister's Webcam Show (Taboo Edition)
Doing Her For Dad (Taboo Edition)
Deceiving Him (The Billionaires' BDSM Sex Club)
Her Brother, Her Hero
Her 'What if' Guy (Pursued By The Billionaire)
The Inheritance: Anything He Craves

Available Now - Themed Singles
Taken By The Team (Humiliation And Gangbang Fantasies Fulfilled)
Taken By The Marines (Humiliation, Gangbang And Cuckold Fantasies Fulfilled)
The Cop And The Girl From The Coffee Shop
The Politician And The Girl From The Coffee Shop
The Assassin And The Girl From The Coffee Shop
The Bounty Hunter And The Girl From The Coffee Shop
The Firefighter And The Girl From The Coffee Shop
The CEO And The Girl From The Coffee Shop
The Porn Star And The Girl From The Coffee Shop

Available Now - Series
Hitching A Ride
Hitching A Ride 2: To Trust A Con
Conjugal Visits
Conjugal Visits 2: New Beginnings
Sibling Rivalry
Sibling Rivalry 2: Never Say Never
Sibling Rivalry 3: In It Together
Moan For Uncle
Moan For Uncle 2: Keeping It Secret
Moan For Uncle 3: No More Secrets
Moan For Uncle 4: Skeletons In The Closet
Moan For Uncle 5: Love Or Duty
Moan For Uncle 6: To Love And Honour
Moan For Hubby (Moan For Uncle 7)

Available Now - Mirror Editions
(Please note Mirror Editions are mainstream non-PI editions of some of Terry's bestselling taboo works.)

Doing Her For The Boss (Rewrite of Doing Her For Dad)
The Marine's Naughty Sister (Rewrite of The Marine's Naughty Neighbour)
The Virgin's Webcam Show (rewrite of Little Virgin Sister's Webcam Show)
Seducing Blake (Rewrite of All For Daddy)

Now Available - Bundles
The Terry Towers' Taboo Collection Vol. 1
The Terry Towers' Taboo Collection Vol. 2
Naughty But Nice Mirror Edition Collection
The Moan For Uncle Bundle (Books 1-3)
The Sibling Rivalry Bundle (Books 1-3)

German Language Versions
Taken By The Team (Humiliation and Gangbang Fantasies Fulfilled)
Von der Mannschaft Durchgenommen (Erniedrigungs- und Gangbangfantasien erfüllt)

Taken By The Marines (Humiliation, Gangbang & Cuckold Fantasies Fulfilled)
Von den Marines durchgenommen (Erniedrigungs- und Gangbang- & Fremdgehfantasien erfüllt)

The Marine's Naughty Sister
Die unanständige Schwester des Marines

Moan For Uncle
Sehnsucht nach dem Onkel

Hitching A Ride: Sexy Anhalter (Anrüchiges einverständnis erotik)

Sibling Rivalry
Geschwister Rivalität

All For Daddy
Alles für Papa

Italian Language Versions
Taken By The Team (Humiliation and Gangbang Fantasies Fulfilled)
Abusata dal gruppo (Umiliazione e Fantasie di Gangbang Soddisfatte)

Moan For Uncle
Un gemito per lo zio

Her Brother, Her Hero
Suo fratello, il suo eroe

Spanish Language Versions

Taken By The Team (Humiliation and Gangbang Fantasies Fulfilled)
Abusada por el equipo (Humillación y fantasías de sexo realizadas en grupo)

Moan For Uncle
El deseo prohibido

French Language Versions
Taken By The Team (Humiliation and Gangbang Fantasies Fulfilled)
Prise Par L'équipe (Fantasmes Assouvis D'humiliation Et De Viol Collectif)

Coming Soon
The Politician And The Girl From The Coffee Shop 2: All That Glitters
The CEO and the Girl From The Coffee Shop 2

Works By Nikki Nexus

Available Now - Singles
Daddy Says: Ménage Sex Games
Santa's Brothel
The Confessional: The Naughty Nuns Series
The Fire Eater
Taken By The Team (Humiliation And Gangbang Fantasies Fulfilled)
Taken By The Marines (Humiliation, Gangbang And Cuckold Fantasies Fulfilled)

Available Now - Bundles
Naughty But Nice Mirror Edition Collection

Coming Soon
Taken By The Mob (Humiliation And Gangbang Fantasies Fulfilled)

German Language Versions
Daddy Says: Ménage Sex Games
Papa sagt:Jetzt ein flotter Dreier

Works By Adrian Athens

Works By Elixa Everett

Midnight Encounter - Seduced By A Vampire
Mitternächtliche Begegnung: Von einem Vampir verführt

Works By Angelique Ambers

Available Now - Singles
Forced Into Submission (Her Fantasy, His Pleasure)

German Language Versions
Forced Into Submission (Her Fantasy, His Pleasure)
Mit Gewalt unterworfen (Ihre Träume, sein Vergnügen)

Excerpt From

The Bounty Hunter
And The Girl From The
Coffee Shop

By

Terry Towers

Chapter 1

Portland, Maine - Day 1

Lincoln had been watching Angelique Donovan - a twenty-eight year old bail jumper - for several days now from the cover of his black 1969 Chevy Impala SS. It wasn't the most inconspicuous car to be on a stakeout in, but it was as close to a partner as he ever got. He'd been given it by his father on his eighteenth birthday - fifteen years ago - just before both of his parents died in a head on collision with a drunk driver.

He had four sisters, though he rarely saw them; life happens like that sometimes and he'd grown to accept that. They all lived in various areas of the North East, while he'd moved to Denver eight years ago and never looked back. For the most part, the car was the closest thing to family that he had and considering he spent more time in it tracking down bail jumpers, than he did in his apartment, he considered the car his home.

The dark-haired beauty was a hard worker, he'd give her that much. She pulled in long shifts every day and of the past three days he'd watched her, two of the shifts had been doubles. Regardless of how many hours she worked, she always greeted each customer with a wide, friendly smile. If he allowed himself he could have easily been pulled in by that bright smile, and the friendly gleam in her lively blue eyes.

But he wouldn't allow himself, because this time next week he'd be handing her over in handcuffs to the authorities in Denver, Colorado, where she was to stand trial on a murder charge. He had wondered countless times over the past few days how such a sweet, pretty little thing like Angelique Donovan could murder anyone. But he'd been a bounty hunter for close to ten years and one thing he'd learned in his time capturing bail jumpers was that anyone is capable of committing a crime. And in many cases it was the people you least expected that committed the worst kinds.

Lincoln sighed. "Well, show-time," he grumbled, thrusting his pistol in his shoulder holster, stuffing a pair of handcuffs in the pocket of his black leather bomber jacket and opening the car door. Not bothering to lock the car, he strutted across the parking lot of the coffee house towards the front entrance, keeping his eyes locked on Angelique.

He wondered if she'd be the type to run when she discovered who he was and why he was there. Most were, but considering it was a public place with so many co-workers around, maybe he'd get lucky and she'd go quietly, maybe even without him having to cuff her.

A guy can only dream.

He opened the front door of the coffee shop for a couple of elderly ladies to exit. They looked up at him, soft smiles touching their lips and muttered their thanks. He gave them a curt nod of his head and slipped through the open door. Of the three girls working the front cashes, Angelique was the only one busy so he waited in line for her.

"I can help you over here, Sir," one of the available hostesses told him but he gave a slight shake of his head.

"Nah thanks, I'll wait for Angelique."

He heard one of the girl mutter 'typical' under her breath followed by, 'she gets all the hot ones.' Lincoln grinned to himself at being referred to as a 'hot one' and removed the mirrored sunglasses that covered his stormy grey eyes and gave the hostess that made the hot one comment a wink. She flushed and scurried away into the back kitchen causing his grin to widen.

The customer before him took his coffee from the counter when Angelique presented him with it and left. His turn. Stepping up to the counter, with his thumbs hooked into the front pockets of his jeans he waited for Angelique to acknowledge him.

"How can I help you?" Angelique looked up, her eyes shining, her smile friendly. She chewed at her lower lip as she waited for his response, drawing his eyes to her full, glossed lips.

His cock stirred in his jeans and he growled at himself for letting his mind become distracted; even if it was just long enough to admire her subtle beauty. Shit, even the dorky visor sitting atop her head looked adorable.

Fuck and double fuck.

He cleared his throat, pushing his attraction for her to the back of his mind. He had a job to do and eyeing her like a teenager with a hard-on wasn't going to get it done. He slipped his hand into the inside pocket of his jacket and pulled out his badge. "Well, Angelique... you could help by coming quietly with me."

He locked gazes with her and waited for it - waiting for the pieces of the puzzle to fall into place for her and for her to realize she'd been tracked down and that she was going to be taken back to Denver.

That's it honey, think it over....

Lincoln held his breath, and before his eyes the realization set in. Her eyes widened, her smile faded, and she took a couple of steps back from the cash register.

Oh come on, don't make me chase you.

But she was going to run; he could see it in her eyes, as they quickly surveyed the restaurant around her. It was the look a deer got when it sensed a hunter and was about to make a run for it. She took another step back.

"I... I th-think you have the wrong person."

Lincoln stuffed the badge back into his inner pocket and then slipped his hand into his outside jacket pocket to produce the handcuffs. "Don't make this harder than it has to be, Angelique."

She sighed. Frowning, her eyes showed a look of resignation. "Alright," she muttered, "I'll go with you."

Slipping the cuffs back into his pocket, Lincoln let out a sigh of relief. He took a step back from the counter and waited for her to come around the counter and allow him to escort her from the restaurant.

Head down, she slowly made her way around the counter, until she hit the door for the kitchen. And just like that she made a run for it, dashing into the kitchen.

"Fuck!" Lincoln growled leaping over the counter and beginning what he assumed would be a short, yet annoying pursuit.

As he entered the kitchen, he felt his feet slip out from under him. He reached out to steady himself on the stainless steel counter next to him, but it was too late. Within seconds he found himself on his back, lying on the greasy floor. He turned his head just in time to see her smirk at him, give a tiny wave and disappear out the back exit.

"Oh, that cocky little..." he bellowed as he pulled himself to his feet and continued his pursuit of her, bursting through the back and into the back lot of the coffee shop. His eyes did a quick scan and happened to see her race into an alley between two apartment buildings.

He broke into a full run chasing after her. He dodged cars as he crossed the busy street and ducked into the alley he'd seen her disappear into. The alley became a maze of dead ends and high fences, so he was certain as long as he followed where it led, he'd have her.

****

Damn, damn, damn.

Tears blurred Angelique's eyes as she sat, hidden at the back of a stinky dumpster. How did life get this bad for her? Just six months ago she had everything, a promising career as a journalist at a prestigious newspaper, a nice home and was soon to be married to a man she loved and admired, Nathan Winters. Then, in the blink of an eye Nathan was dead and *she* was the one going to trial for his murder.

Her breath caught in her throat as she heard the sound of footsteps beside the dumpster. Just as the footsteps began to move away, she heard a squeak and felt something run across her exposed ankle. She yelped, and covered her mouth to try and stifle the noise, but it was too late. The owner of the footsteps started back in her direction.

The footsteps came back to the dumpster, and the lid was flipped open to display the bounty hunter glaring down at her. In other circumstances she would have found him attractive, but as he stood staring down at her trembling body, all she could thing about was that this was the end of the line for her. She was going to trial and then to prison for a crime she didn't commit.

"It's over Angelique, come out." He extended his hand to her, but she cowered away from him, inching away until her back hit the cold steel back of the massive dumpster.

The blonde-haired man huffed and his eyes narrowed at her. "You can't be serious. You have *no* idea how pissed I'm going to be if I have to come in there after you."

It may have been over for her; she was caught, but she'd be damned if she was going to make it easy on him. She cocked her head to the side and gave him the same condescending smirk she'd given him when she'd seen him slip on the vegetable oil she'd intentionally spilled on the kitchen floor during her escape from the coffee shop. "Guess you're going to have to earn that bounty and come and get me."

His features darkened and anger flashed within his deep grey eyes. "Fine. Have it your way." A deep, growl-like noise came from him as he pulled himself up and into the dumpster.

Seeing one final chance to escape, she scrambled to her feet and leapt over the side as he jumped in. She tripped as she landed on the cement ground of the alleyway, skinning the palms of her hands, but she righted herself once more and lunged forward.

"For the love of fuck, Angelique!" he shouted after her followed by a grunt and thud as he jumped from the dumpster and continued his pursuit.

She had just begun to regain a small sliver of hope when she felt an arm wrap around her waist and an impact which felt like the force of a Mack truck slamming into her back, sending her tumbling to the ground. As Angelique landed, the wind was knocked from her as his weight came crashing down onto her. She was still trying to regain her breath when she felt his weight lift, and her wrists being grabbed roughly and cuffed behind her back.

"We could have just done this the easy way, Angelique and you could have saved me a lot of aggravation. Now you have me in a bad mood."

Angelique huffed. "Do you honestly think I care about your mood?"

"You should since you're stuck with me for the next week. I can be a really nice guy, Angelique, but I can just as easily be a major asshole. Ball's in your court."

Once her arms were secure, Lincoln stood, grabbed her arm and pulled her roughly to her feet. Still not wanting to admit defeat, even with her arms secure behind her back, she tried to jerk her arm from his grasp.

Grabbing her around the waist he pulled her rear tight against him. The fight in her was pretty much gone, but she couldn't resist bucking against him a couple more times. She gasped and she froze against him as she felt his cock begin to grow and press against her bottom.

"Oh-my-god," she gasped. "You're actually turned on by this? By chasing down a defenceless woman?"

Lincoln stepped back from her, grabbed her arm roughly and pulled her along as they made their way back out of the alleyway. "You were squirming that tight ass of yours against my dick as if you were a damned stripper after a buck; what did you expect?" he defended, refusing to meet her gaze, though as she watched his expression she saw a flush beginning to redden his face. A slight grin touched her lips as a plan began to formulate in her mind, not the best plan in the world, admittedly, but one nonetheless.

She allowed her eyes to wander up and down the length of him. He was at least six foot. She guessed close to 6 foot 2, short-cut blonde hair and deep grey eyes. His shoulders and chest were thick and powerful. He was attractive, no doubt about it, in a rugged sort of way. The kind of guy she'd easily be able to fall for - under different circumstances.